AT THE EDGE OF THE WOODS

Also available by Victoria Houston

The Loon Lake/Lew Ferris Mysteries

Wolf Hollow

Hidden in the Pines

The Loon Lake Fishing Mysteries

Nonfiction Titles

AT THE EDGE
OF THE WOODS

A Lew Ferris
Mystery

VICTORIA HOUSTON

CROOKED
LANE

NEW YORK

Copyright © 2024 by Victoria Houston

Published in the United States by Crooked Lane Books, an imprint of The Quick Brown Fox & Company LLC.

Crooked Lane Books and its logo are trademarks of The Quick Brown Fox & Company LLC.

Library of Congress Catalog-in-Publication data available upon request.

ISBN (hardcover): 978-1-63910-653-0
ISBN (ebook): 978-1-63910-654-7

Cover design by Jerry Todd

Printed in the United States.

www.crookedlanebooks.com

Crooked Lane Books
34 West 27th St., 10th Floor
New York, NY 10001

First Edition: April 2024

10 9 8 7 6 5 4 3 2 1

For my new Wisconsin neighbors—Nicole, Jason, and Vesper

How secret are even the open lives of others!
—Laurie Colwin, "Evensong," *The New Yorker*,
April 17, 2023

Chapter One

The early September morning held a slight chill as Bert Willoughby slammed shut the door of his Range Rover and strode onto the broken cement of the decaying tennis court. Robin Carpenter, his pickleball partner, had already arrived.

"Had to chase two turkeys off this morning," she called out with a grin as he walked toward her.

"Not a bad day to practice," said Bert, setting down his bag and reaching to set up the pickleball net he had rolled up under a tarp on the old court. The tennis court had seen frequent activity years earlier when the boys' camp, established in the 1920s, thrived with campers from Chicago and Detroit, but it had seldom been used since. Bert had bought the property and hired a local firm to pave a section wide enough and long enough to provide a safe surface that he and Robin could practice on. It was hidden from the prying eyes of their competitors and kept cool by the protective leaves of the birches and oaks the former owners of the camp had left standing.

"Smartest twenty-acre investment I ever made," Bert would brag to friends who wondered why someone would buy the old place. After all, the lodge was set so far back from the Loon Lake shoreline that it had minimal appeal for anyone looking for a lakefront setting. "Great for pickleball, for hunting, and who knows—someday I may rebuild that old lodge."

When the sixty-eight-year-old dentist had finished setting up the pickleball net, he and Robin started batting the ball back and forth, loosening up. They were expecting two other players to join them for a practice session any minute. As Bert batted the ball, he applauded himself for staying so fit into his late sixties. No wonder Robin was attracted to him. He smiled to himself.

The air was still, with no wind. The lake, fifty yards away down a slight embankment, was so serene that conversations carried from the fishing boats anchored near the far shore.

Pop, pop, pop went the pickleball from racket to racket. Sun peeked through the leaves overhead, dappling the court.

Robin, racket ready, heard a different sound: a *muffled* pop. She watched the man across the net falter, then fall.

To her it sounded like the pop of death.

Chapter Two

The woman who strode toward the man leaning over the still form sprawled on the old tennis court wore a khaki uniform that emphasized her wide shoulders and sturdy build. The expression on her face, under a cap of dark-brown natural curls trimmed to stay out of her eyes, was grim.

She had been enjoying her second cup of coffee a quarter mile away at the home of the dear friend with whom she had spent the night when she received an emergency alert from her department's switchboard. The location was too close for her to wait on the Loon Lake police to arrive.

"Homicide, Chief." The statement from the man crouched over the body was delivered with an air of authority that angered the woman wearing the badge.

"Pecore, you are not qualified to make that determination. And for the record, I am not your chief. I'm the sheriff," she said through gritted teeth. McBride County sheriff Lew Ferris had no respect for Ed Pecore, the county coroner. He had been appointed by his brother-in-law, mayor of the town of Loon Lake—an appointment based on a set of remarkable qualifications that included twenty-one years of running a bat-infested tavern preceded by eight years of bartending and two stints in the city jail for DUIs. But in the Northwoods of Wisconsin, coroners are appointed, not elected, and he was the mayor's brother-in-law.

*　*　*

About to turn fifty-three, Lew Ferris had been elected county sheriff after serving as chief of the Loon Lake Police for fifteen years. She was the first woman to have held both positions in the Northwoods, and with years of experience dealing with Ed Pecore, she didn't hesitate to challenge the man she considered so inept he could be dangerous.

"Pecore, what makes you think he didn't have a heart attack?" she asked.

"See for yourself," said Pecore in a smug voice. It was clear he was tickled that he was about to be proven right for once.

After walking back to her cruiser for a pair of nitrile gloves, Lew came back, knelt, and gently pushed at the victim's upper body. He had fallen forward with his head bent, obscuring the blood beginning to pool beneath him.

"I see," said Lew, getting to her feet. "It appears he's been shot, all right. But we still can't call it homicide, Ed. That's for the Wausau boys to determine," she said, using the term locals used for the Wausau Crime Lab investigators.

"I don't see why the hell I can't say what's obvious," said Ed, blurting his words out with anger. "Bullets don't lie."

"Ed," said Lew in a calm voice, "people are sighting their rifles for deer season. Who's to say this wasn't an accident? It can happen. I know from experience." The fact that there was no exit wound suggested the bullet had come from a distance, which to her suggested an accident rather than a deliberate killing.

She didn't say more and Pecore didn't ask, but she would never forget an afternoon in her teens when her father, who had been sighting his deer rifle in their backyard, pulled the trigger and accidentally grazed the head of a bird hunter pursuing a partridge through aspen a good half mile away. The hunter survived, but Lew and her father made a pact never to sight a rifle anywhere than at a rifle range.

Looking up from where she was kneeling by the victim, Lew saw a small crowd gathering. She wasn't surprised. The homes and cottages along the road leading to the camp were seldom disturbed by sirens, and hers had been screaming when she sped by on her way to the old summer camp. Who wouldn't be curious?

Reaching for her cell phone, she called Todd Donovan, her former colleague who had replaced her as chief of the Loon Lake Police. While she was telling him where she was and why, she took a closer look at the victim's face and recognized the man.

"Todd, it's Bert Willoughby. We're going to have press all over this, especially as we have an unknown cause of death. I'll put in a call to the Wausau boys ASAP. How soon can you get here?" Hearing that he was in the middle of working a serious car accident, she added, "Okay, don't worry about this. I'll ask the witness a few questions, then notify Mrs. Willoughby. I'll stay here until Roger can secure the crime scene," she said, referring to Officer Adamczyk, who was also on duty that morning.

She looked over at the other person on the court. The woman, athletic looking with short, straight blond hair and wearing tennis shorts and a T-shirt, had been standing back. As Lew continued to examine the victim, the blonde muttered something into Pecore's ear. It was obvious they knew each other.

After putting her cell phone away, Lew turned to the woman. "Why did you call the coroner and not 911? How do you know Mr. Pecore?"

"Um, Ed's my uncle," said the blonde, sounding defensive. "He told me a long time ago that if I ever found a dead body to call him right away. Right, Uncle Ed?" She glanced at the man Lew considered a weasel, who gave a shrug.

"But I was kind of kidding, honey," said Pecore. He looked as if he was expecting a reprimand.

"But that's his job, isn't it?" The blonde's face had tightened. "Did I do the wrong thing?" She threw her uncle a worried look.

Lew checked her off as not overly bright. "How did you know he was dead?" She worked hard to keep her tone even. "Are you a physician? A nurse?"

The woman shook her head. "He wasn't breathing, and his eyes were, y'know, just kinda open."

"That doesn't mean he might not have been able to be resuscitated . . ." As she was speaking, Lew shook her head.

Whoever said idiocy doesn't run in families? She gave up. "All right. Please, tell me your name and why you and the victim are here and when exactly this happened." She didn't have to ask the name of the victim. She knew it was Dr. Bertram Willoughby, the head of a local dental clinic and a wealthy Loon Lake resident.

"I'm Robin Carpenter," the woman said. "I just moved back here about six months ago. Bert and I are pickleball partners, and we've been practicing for a big tournament in Wausau next weekend." Her voice faltered as she added, "Yeah . . . partners. That's what we were." A tear slipped down one cheek.

Lew could see the woman growing more emotional by the moment. "I understand. You were close to Bert . . ."

"Not legally," said Robin, her voice catching in a sob and pressing her right index finger against her lips. Lew waited. "I'm not sure how to handle this." As she ducked her head and turned away, Lew could barely hear her say, "He's still married to Jane."

"Ah," said Lew, aware that several bystanders had edged close enough to overhear her questioning. "Tell you what, Miss Carpenter, follow me so we can talk with more privacy."

"It's *missus*," said the woman, "I'm divorced." She followed Lew across a dirt lane to the top of a grassy hill overlooking the lake.

When they were a safe distance from curious neighbors, Lew asked, "Does Mrs. Willoughby know about you? Is that what you're telling me? I'm only asking because I have to notify Dr. Willoughby's family."

Robin took a deep breath before squinting her eyes as she said, "He was planning to tell her he wanted a divorce this next week. He's been pulling together his finances and stuff before telling her."

"I see. So the current Mrs. Willoughby is next of kin."

"Yes."

As they were talking, Lew could hear muffled pops coming from the Loon Lake Rifle Range, a private club located across the lake.

"Wait—hear that?" Robin gave a startled yelp. "That's what I heard before Bert fell over. That's who shot him." She yanked at Lew's arm and dropped to her knees. *"Hit the ground—"*

"No." Lew pulled away from her. "There's no danger. Those noises are from the rifle range across the lake and quite far away. The sound carries, but no one shoots in this direction." She helped the woman up to her feet. "You're safe."

"But that's what I heard. A pop just like that."

Robin's eyes were so wide with fear, Lew didn't doubt her. What she did doubt was that a bullet from the well-regulated rifle range had been what took Bert Willoughby down.

At the sound of footsteps, Lew turned to see a man running toward them. Lew tried to motion for him to stay back.

"No, no, Sheriff," he called. "I live right down the road, and I know who did this."

Chapter Three

⌒

Lew stared at the man who had run up. Short and stocky with a carefully trimmed moustache, he was so agitated he bounced even as he tried to stand still.

"Sir, I'm sure you have good information, and I'll be with you in a moment," said Lew, motioning for him to stay back. If she had learned anything in her years of law enforcement, it was that there was always a bystander convinced they knew "the whole story." This guy fit the profile.

"No, wait, Sheriff, something you should know," said the man, ignoring her. "One of the neighbors here—not me, I'm fine with pickleball, but Larry Weston . . ." He paused to wave towards a house behind him. "He owns that big new A-frame next door to the camp property. He's been furious with Dr. Willoughby for being out here at five, six in the morning batting that damn ball around."

Again Lew tried to shut him down. "I hear you, and I'll be right with you." It didn't work.

"I saw him drive off just before you got here, Sheriff, and—"

The guy was relentless, Lew thought. "All right, fella." She gave up, put both hands on her hips, and stared at him. "Just who are you, and what are you implying? Because you can get yourself into a lot of trouble making false accusations."

"I heard him up at the Loon Lake Bar, and I'm saying he's been very, very angry—"

"Yes," said Robin, jumping into the conversation. "I know who he's talking about. And, boy, did that man rant. Shouting and screaming—just *screaming*—at me and Bert." She gave an emphatic nod of her head. "Two mornings ago." Her enthusiasm added a coarseness to her features, reminding Lew of Pecore, the woman's uncle.

From the corner of her eye, Lew saw a Loon Lake Police squad car pull up next to the old tennis court. Excusing herself, she ran over to make sure Roger Adamczyk knew exactly how much of the area to secure.

A failed insurance salesman who had opted ten years ago to join the Loon Lake Police, thinking he could earn his retirement giving out parking tickets, Roger Adamczyk required specific directions on how to handle anything other than a parking violation. While his real talent lay in taking shortcuts, he had proven to be kind to his colleagues in the department. So Lew put up with him. When she was convinced he was capable of securing what might be a crime scene—though she continued to suspect it wasn't—she hurried back to Robin and the man who was such a pest.

"You"—she pointed to the man—"I want you to tell Officer Adamczyk everything you think may have happened. Once he has cordoned off the tennis court over there, he'll be ready to take down your information. I told him you may be a key witness."

That seemed to satisfy the guy. Lew checked her watch. She needed to contact the Wausau boys before she missed getting on their schedule for the day—at least the *right* schedule, that of one of their top investigators, who happened to be a good friend and one of her best fly-fishing students.

Looking over at Bert's pickleball partner, she said, "Robin, please meet me in my office in two hours. One of the investigators from the Wausau Crime Lab will be there to assist me in documenting what you saw and heard when Dr. Willoughby was shot."

Once in her cruiser and heading in the direction of the Willoughby home, Lew called Bruce Peters's personal cell number. It rang four times before she heard his familiar voice.

"Yo there, Sheriff Ferris, got a hatch going? My double haul is itching to hit that Prairie River, doncha know? Practiced all weekend."

Bruce Peters was a talented forensic scientist who loved to fly-fish. Once he'd met Lewellyn Ferris, then the Loon Lake chief of police, who moonlighted as a fly-fishing instructor on her off days, he had made it a point to trade putting in overtime for free instruction in the trout stream.

It worked for Lew. She had loved fishing ever since she'd grown up with a grandfather who owned a sporting goods shop and brought her along when he stole hours in the trout stream. And knowing a forensic scientist like Bruce allowed her, when needed, to work around the director of the crime lab, a man who never failed to let her know that "in my humble opinion, a woman is putting herself at unnecessary risk working in law enforcement." His bias was unmistakable.

Just as unmistakable was Bruce's love for his fly rod and the world that opened to him when he was with Lew. A tall, stalwart man, he had dark bushy eyebrows that had a life of their own, jumping up and down when he laughed—and he laughed often. Lew liked to swear she could hear his eyebrows levitate over the cell phone.

"No sighting of blue-winged olives this morning," she said, referring to an insect genus beloved by trout, "but we have until October fifteenth, so who knows? Right now I have a puzzle that may well be an accidental shooting, but I need your help, Bruce. Any chance you can make it up here in a couple hours? I have a witness who was nearby when the individual was shot—"

"Sure," Bruce said, interrupting. "You picked a good day—only two meth busts and one domestic violence. My colleagues can handle those."

Lew breathed a sigh of relief. "Terrific. See you in my office. Let me know when you have an ETA."

"This is the new office, right?"

"Sure is. We moved into our new building since you and I worked together last. Same coffeepot—I'll have a cup waiting."

* * *

Now the hard part, thought Lew as she turned off the high-way toward the town of Loon Lake. She knew the Willoughby house. Everyone did. The lovely redbrick house dated from the 1930s, when one of the managers of the paper mill had built it. The original owner had liked to brag that his architect had worked for the Rhinelanders, the family that brought the first train to the region in the late 1800s.

Bert and his wife had made improvements but stayed true to the contemporary feel of the house. No doubt it cost a fortune to maintain with the original windows and shutters, but it had been designated as a historic preservation site by the local historical society, so Loon Lake residents assumed Bert got a nice tax deduction for his tasteful efforts. But maybe it was his wife who wanted the authenticity and they hadn't been looking for a tax break.

Lew had no idea. All she knew for sure was that it was never, ever pleasant to deliver heartbreaking news.

* * *

The woman who answered the door was wearing a loose man's shirt over baggy tan jeans—which failed to hide a bulging midriff—and her short legs and long arms waving made her look comical.

"Mrs. Willoughby?" asked Lew, wondering if she could be the family housekeeper.

"No, no, I'm not expecting a delivery." Spidery arms gestured for Lew to scram. "You must have the wrong house."

"I'm not delivering anything. I'm Sheriff Lewellyn Ferris," said Lew, her voice firm as she held up her ID.

"Oh, sorry," said the woman, blinking as she turned away. "Where on earth are my glasses? I am so sorry." She reached for a pair of glasses on a side table in the hall behind her. Turning back, she peered at Lew. "Oh, I am so sorry, Sheriff Ferris. Is something wrong? I checked with the city inspector to be sure our new fence met code . . ."

"Are you Mrs. Willoughby?"

"Yes, of course. Who else could I be?"

"May I come inside, please? I'm afraid I have some disturbing news."

* * *

Lew wasn't surprised when Jane Willoughby sat silent on the sofa across from her as she explained what had happened. Over the years, Lew had learned that the unexpected death of a loved one triggered one of two responses: an explosion of anguish or, more often, a flat sense of disbelief. For this woman, it was the latter. Mrs. Willoughby was at first insistent that her husband could not have been shot, but after Lew repeated the news several times, it finally seemed to sink in.

As Lew waited for the moment when she could suggest that the woman call her family so she could take her leave, she glanced around the area where she was sitting. She saw a wide hallway leading toward the rear of the house and assumed there would be a dining room and a kitchen nearby. A wide carpeted stairway led up to a second floor.

Looking past the stairway, she saw what appeared to be a den with a large antique wooden desk off to one side and facing an entire wall of guns. Some of the guns were displayed on wooden racks, others in open cases set on shelves.

As she stood to leave, she paused at the entrance to the den for a closer look. There were guns of all types—rifles, shotguns, handguns.

Jane, having finally appeared ready to accept the news and call her family, began to walk Lew to the door. "So Dr. Willoughby was a hunter," commented Lew.

"Oh, no, he didn't hunt," said Jane. "Not anymore, anyway. We hunted when we were young, but for the last twenty years . . ." She paused, and pride edged into her voice as she said, "Bert was a *collector*. Some of these guns are worth thousands of dollars. And Bert has . . . had . . . many more in our house in Jackson Hole too. He loved showing them off. He dusted them himself, you know." She paused as she looked more closely at Lew.

"Say, aren't you the woman Doc Osborne . . . ?" She didn't finish her question, but the expression in her eyes was disapproving. "I knew Mary Lee. You know—his late wife. Lovely woman. She had class." Her implication was clear—Mary Lee had been far superior to Lew, and Lew had no business even thinking of being involved with Doc Osborne.

"Yes," said Lew in a matter-of-fact tone. "Dr. Osborne is my student. I teach fly-fishing when I can grab a little time." She gave Jane Willoughby a prim smile as she pulled the door closed behind her.

Chapter Four

Jane watched the woman walk back to the SUV marked SHERIFF on the side. "*That* is the woman Paul Osborne has been seeing?" she muttered to herself. "What is he thinking?"

She had vivid memories of her late bridge partner. You never saw Mary Lee Osborne in anything but the most tailored, expensive clothes—slacks and skirts and cashmere sweaters—that fit her tiny, slender figure so well that Jane couldn't help the envy she felt every time they got together. And her home? "Exquisite taste" was what the bridge girls would exclaim after leaving the Osborne house on the nights that Mary Lee hosted.

Whatever it was that had attracted Paul Osborne to that tough-looking cop in a man's uniform, Jane could not imagine. *Fishing* together? *Excuse me?* What kind of woman attracted a man with a fishing rod and night crawlers? They must both be nuts.

After stewing over the image of Mary Lee's handsome widowed husband spending time with a woman who wore men's clothing and whose hair was too long and curly, Jane realized she had better make a phone call.

* * *

"Katherine, this is Mom—"

"Sorry, Mom, I'm with a patient. Call you right back," said her daughter. From the note of frustration in Katherine's voice, Jane could tell she must be leaning to speak into her Apple watch.

"Your dad's dead." As she spoke, Jane made sure to keep relief out of her voice. She had to sound grief-stricken. She knew exactly what would happen next: Katherine would pause and stare at her wrist.

"What did you say?" her daughter asked.

"Your dad is dead. He was out practicing his pickleball at the old boys' camp, and someone shot him."

* * *

After a pause, Katherine stepped back from her patient and walked out to the lobby, where she told her father's dental assistant, Robin Steadman, the news. "I have to get home to Mom," she added, pulling off her surgical gloves.

"Ohmygosh, of course you do," said Robin, sounding stunned as she jumped to her feet from the desk, where she had been working on a computer. "Don't worry, I'll take care of your patient."

"Thank you. I was just finishing up." Katherine spoke as she was heading out the door.

"Please call me when you know more," said Robin. "Patients will be upset. I'm upset. I don't believe this."

* * *

Driving to her mother's house, Katherine had mixed feelings. Growing up, she had worked hard at doing what she thought might make her father care for her as much as she loved him. But closeness between them had proven so elusive that she'd eventually given up. The day she realized her parents weren't particularly close to each other helped her deal with his lack of interest in who she was. And because she had learned to live with the distance between them, she wasn't feeling as devastated at the news of his death as some daughters might.

Though she had followed in her father's footsteps to become a dentist, she had chosen the profession not so much because she loved the practice and the science but more because it was, as she'd told a close girlfriend, "one hell of a way to make money—beats internal medicine, that's for sure."

As she had become proficient, she'd begun to realize what a lazy professional her father was. Only recently he had barely avoided a malpractice suit when he'd ignored a patient's life-threatening oral infection—or misinterpreted the X-rays. She wasn't sure which, but she now had a good idea of how often his careful, experienced dental assistant, Robin, had caught and corrected his errors.

And that in spite of the fact that he paid his staff as little as possible along with refusing to provide health benefits. The latter was one big reason, Katherine had recently learned, that he earned so much money. She hadn't yet

decided if—when, as planned, she took over the practice—
she would cover employee health benefits. The financial
advantage of cutting that cost might be too tempting.

Only rarely would she admit that she just might be her
father's daughter.

*   *   *

Jane was waiting for her in the kitchen with a freshly brewed
pot of coffee. "I want to talk to you before I call our lawyer."

"Or a therapist? Mom, you must be feeling awful—"

"You're kidding, right? You know your father and I
could barely get along. I know this sounds terrible, but I
have spent the last ten years of my life hoping, wishing the
man would die of a heart attack." She shook a finger at
Katherine. "Don't you dare tell me I'm a bad person. At
least I'm honest. Do you have any idea how many of my
friends would love to get out of their marriages? Do you?"

Katherine blinked. "But a lawyer, Mom? Shouldn't we
be calling, like, the hospital or the funeral home or the
police?" What she didn't say was shouldn't they at least pre-
tend to be saddened by their loss?

"No, the lawyer. I want to know our family financial
position—your father refused to ever talk to me about
money. He said it was none of my business and as long as I
had what I needed to just shut up. Well, I need to know if
we're destitute, right?"

"Mom, you know better than that," said Katherine with
a forced laugh. "I'm sure you're worth more than you ever
imagined. Making money was Dad's passion."

"He's always been mean about it, KK, and you know it." Jane spat out the words even as she called her daughter by her childhood nickname.

Katherine wasn't surprised. She was used to her parents' contentious style of marriage. Whereas some couples thrived on friendship, frustration and anger seemed to fuel the bond between Bert and Jane. It didn't help that Katherine's mother had the bad habit of getting so angry that she would refuse midargument to finish what she was saying or, even worse, refuse to listen to what the other person was trying to say.

"Mom, please tell me exactly what happened," said Katherine, after she sat down across from her mother at the kitchen table.

"I told you once," said Jane, slamming her coffee cup down on the table, half of it spilling on the tabletop. "How often do I have to repeat myself, for Chrissake?"

This was more volatile than usual for her mother, Katherine thought. "You said he was playing—"

"Yeah, playing pickleball with that goddamn Robin—"

"Robin? No, Mom, Robin's in the office. I just—"

"*I know Robin*, goddammit. That's it. I'm done. You want to know more? Call that stupid sheriff woman."

Jane threw her coffee cup in the sink, where it shattered, and stomped out of the room. "Going to the lawyer's office," she called back to her daughter. "Coming?"

Katherine sighed, checked her phone for messages, and got to her feet to follow her mother. In silence. She had learned long ago that the only way to manage this woman was to keep your mouth shut.

Chapter Five

The new building housing the sheriff's department and county jail had been built across the road from St. Mary's Hospital. Here, unlike at the stately courthouse, where Lew could admire the ancient oaks and sweeping lawn surrounding the historic building as she pulled into her parking spot, she was met with black asphalt and yellow lines upon arrival.

"Nothing like the warmth of an office park," she muttered to herself as she got out of the cruiser to push her way through the wide glass doors fronting the sheriff's department. Whereas she used to pass by Marlaine on dispatch and greet her in person, now she nodded to the two women hunkered down behind a protective glass wall. Life had changed.

Once in her office, she felt a little more at home. She had insisted on keeping her old oak desk from the police department and the small rectangular wood table that held the ancient Mr. Coffee machine. Some things didn't have to change.

Walking in right behind her with a carafe of water to pour into the Mr. Coffee was her senior admin, Judith Hanson. "Hey, I can do that," said Lew, reaching for the carafe. "Making coffee is not your job."

"Not yours either," said the older woman with a grin. "I'm the one desperate for an extra cup this morning—so, yes, it is my job. At least for the moment."

Lew chuckled and stepped back to let her pour.

"And thank you for that early brief on the Willoughby death this morning," said Judith as she scooped ground coffee into the basket. "Right after your alert came in, I got calls from both the television and radio stations. I told them you would have an update later this morning. Let me know when you want me to set up a press conference."

"Not until noon at the earliest. I'm expecting Bruce Peters by nine thirty, and I want him to see the crime scene and talk to our one witness before I say anything definitive."

"Just say when." Judith clicked the coffeepot's ON button.

* * *

Judith Hanson had originally been hired to help Dani Wright, the Loon Lake Police Department's IT expert. Once Lew was elected sheriff, however, she wasted no time poaching Dani to provide IT services to the county and promoting Judith to the position of senior administrator for the department. Lew was well aware that the two women brought both diligence and humor to their positions, helping to make the sheriff's department an efficient as well as pleasant place to work. And Lew insisted that behind closed doors her colleagues call her by her first name and not her title. No one objected.

The smile that had crossed Judith's face as she poured herself a cup of coffee faded. Instead of heading back to her own office, she set her cup down on Lew's desk and crossed her arms as she said in a blunt tone, "Thought you better know we already have an anonymous tip on who may have killed Bert Willoughby. Phoned in twenty minutes ago."

"Really," said Lew, pulling out her chair and turning on her computer. "News travels fast in a small town. What kind of a tip?" She glanced over at Judith. "I'm not sure Willoughby's death wasn't an accident. This is peak season for sighting deer rifles. Here in Wisconsin we must get two or three accidental shootings every deer season. Too many careless people."

"The caller offered to share the name of someone they know who might want Bert Willoughby dead," said Judith, her voice even. "Once they told me why, I have to say I sympathize, even though I'm sure they're wrong. I wrote the name down, but I doubt you're interested."

"You're right—I'm not," said Lew. "The caller sounds like a neighborhood busybody. Do you agree?"

"I do, and I'll tell you why: not only did I grow up here, but I went through junior high and high school with Bert Willoughby, and I know half a dozen people who might want him dead. Of course, most of them are likely to have passed away themselves by now." She gave a rueful grin. "Guess that tells you how old I am, doesn't it."

"He was that unpleasant a guy?" asked Lew. "I don't really know the man, though I've heard the name. When I was working at the mill years ago and my kids were young, Doc Osborne was our family dentist and the only dentist I knew, since I grew up in Tomahawk," she said, naming a small town twenty miles west of Loon Lake. "I'm afraid I'm not that familiar with Loon Lake families and their dysfunctional histories."

"Well, I am," said Judith. "My father practiced medicine at the same time Bert's father opened his practice in Loon Lake. Doc Osborne's father was practicing then too, so he'll know about this, I'm sure. My dad was not impressed with Dr. Willoughby Senior. Found him to be a blowhard and very careless—Dad called him slovenly—in his practice. One of my mother's friends changed dentists after watching old man Willoughby move from one patient's chair to the next without washing his hands. Made her feel like throwing up."

"I can imagine," said Lew. "By today's standards, that's not just unhealthy—it's criminal."

"Our tipster this morning has a worse story." Judith had settled into the chair across from Lew, and she sipped her coffee before continuing. "The person on the phone said they're a family friend of a man who died of cancer because Bert pooh-poohed his symptoms and refused to send him to a specialist for a second opinion. By the time the individual was diagnosed, he was stage four, with only a few months to live. So the caller thinks someone in that family might be out for revenge."

"A little too obvious," said Lew, raising an eyebrow.

"I agree," said Judith. "But telling the story at least made the caller feel better."

A soft knock sounded on the door, and the face Lew had last seen when he brought her coffee in bed that morning appeared.

"Got one cup left?" asked the man whose appearance could ease her day, no matter how difficult things might be.

* * *

Dr. Paul Osborne was the reason Lew's morning office routine hadn't changed since her election. Unless a tornado hit town, she kept the time open for one last cup of coffee in her office with Osborne after he'd spent an hour or more around a Formica-topped table at McDonald's. But it wasn't *just* a table where he had his early-morning coffee—it was a table shared with five men he had known for over thirty years, including two from childhood. Three were fishing buddies, one also a retired dentist and two, like Osborne, were widowers. And all somehow had access to better gossip than anything on the internet.

Who needs deputies when you got Doc's McDonald's crowd? Lew had cracked more than once.

"Sit down, Doc," she said as Judith stood up to leave. "No, Judith, stay, please. If anyone knows who might want to kill Bert Willoughby, it'll be one of the guys in Doc's coffee crew."

"True," said Osborne, trying to repress a smile he knew was inappropriate. "Got a list of six possibilities."

"Serious?" asked Lew.

"No. But I do know two people who certainly have good reason, though they would never do such a thing."

"Let's talk about it," said Lew, checking her watch. "Bruce Peters will be here shortly, but I'd like to hear what people are saying."

Osborne walked over to the Mr. Coffee, where he found his usual cup waiting. He took his time pouring, apparently relishing the anticipation he could feel building behind him. He turned, walked over to Lew's desk, and took the chair alongside Judith.

"I would say that Dick made the best case for who would want to shoot the guy," said Doc, referring to a retired banker with whom he had grown up. "Dick worked closely with Bill Oliver of Oliver Investments on trust-related investments up until Bill passed last year . . ."

"Yes?" Lew egged him on.

"Bill told Dick that he had put Bert into Apple when it launched at six dollars a share—"

"*Six dollars a share?*" Stunned, Judith interrupted.

"I'm exaggerating," said Osborne with a wave of one hand, "but Bill said he and Bert were in the same deer camp and he urged him to invest in Apple and several other stocks. Bert followed his advice, which paid off quite nicely. When Bert sold—again at Bill's urging—he made well over a million dollars." Osborne paused. "Then Bert refused to pay Bill a penny of commission."

Judith made a dismissive sound. "That sounds like the Bert I grew up with," she said. "Mean son of a bitch."

"Bill said that Bert alleged—and these are Bert's words—'Any idiot could have made those trades, and you advised me as a friend, not a client. You know that, Bill.' So he just refused to pay the man who had advised him over the years. Bill said Bert was the only person over his entire career who stiffed him." Osborne sipped his coffee before adding, "Bill figured he was owed nearly two hundred grand on the Apple investment alone. He considered taking the guy to court but had a stroke before he could."

"You said there are two people who might have reason to want Bert dead." Lew spoke in a quiet voice.

"Yes, I did, and this is one sad story too. Bert has had a caretaker for years whom you may remember, Judith. Did you ever know Denny Worth?"

"Yes, he was in my class too. Quiet, sweet guy."

"Well, Denny did everything for Bert—repairs on his office buildings in Loon Lake and Rhinelander; on his houses, including the one here and his winter place in Jackson Hole. He did everything from yardwork to changing lightbulbs.

"I know from his daughter, Sue Davenport, that Bert never paid Denny more than minimum wage and no health benefits. About two years before he died last year, Denny started having stomach issues. Sue urged him to see a doctor, but he refused. She said he told her he couldn't afford it and he knew he'd feel better soon. One day she stopped by his trailer home and found him in agony, so she rushed him to the emergency room . . ."

"I don't want to hear this," said Judith, dropping her head.

"Stage-four colon cancer," said Osborne. "Gone in four months. Bert did visit him in the hospital."

"Wow." Lew shook her head.

"The boys I knew growing up didn't like Bert because he cheated," said Judith. "Especially on the tennis court."

"*That* hasn't changed," said Osborne with a grim laugh.

"Herm's son-on-law, who has been teaching pickleball, said Bert has been notorious for entering regional doubles tournaments saying that he and his partner are intermediate players when everyone knows they're hands down expert at the game."

"Small potatoes compared to what Bert did to Bill Oliver or Denny Worth, but certainly irritating to people involved with the sport. That would be like our friend Ray Pradt entering a muskie tournament alleging he's a beginner," said Osborne, referring to his neighbor and close friend, who held a national ranking in the muskie-fishing world. "Can you imagine Ray pulling such a stunt?"

"No," said Lew with a laugh. "How would he have time? Ray's too busy pulling other stunts, like charming Dani into editing his podcast for free."

"Really? I'll talk to her about *that*," said Judith. "Excuse me, this has been very interesting, Doc, but I better get back to my office and more tipsters."

"My friends had a lot more to say about Bert," said Osborne, "but that gives you an idea who the guy was. That plus he ran a dental office that looked like a high school gym, with linoleum floors and chairs lined up side by side so there was no privacy. Bert liked the bucks, and he made the bucks."

Lew reached for his empty coffee cup. As Osborne got to his feet, she asked one final question: "So, Doc, the man died rich, but did he die happy?"

"That's the question," said Osborne, and turned to leave her office.

"Wait, one last thing," said Lew. "I had to meet with Jane Willoughby this morning and give her the news. I got the impression she was a good friend of your late wife's . . ."

Osborne paused. "That woman. Yes, they were friends. Close? I'm not sure. Not sure Mary Lee was close to anyone—except Mallory," he said, referring to his oldest daughter.

Osborne stood in the doorway, a thoughtful look on his face. Lew had a good idea what he must be thinking.

*   *   *

Paul Osborne had been married to Mary Lee for nearly thirty years before her death from bronchitis that had turned deadly in the midst of a blizzard. And as someone whose mother had died when he was six and whose father had never remarried, he hadn't known what to expect in a relationship between a man and a woman.

Until he met Lewellyn Ferris while taking a beginner's lesson in fly-fishing, he hadn't known that lovers could also be friends. His marriage to Mary Lee had followed a pattern he had observed in a few other marriages: a lack of ardor after the birth of the planned number of children, criticism of the pastime he loved most ("How much more of our money will you waste on that damn fishing boat, Paul?") and criticism of his career ("Paul, dentists in Milwaukee make a lot more money than you do here in stupid Loon Lake—I don't understand why you can't sell your dad's practice so we can live in a much nicer community"). Other than voicing her irritation with him over their years together, his wife had had little else to say—at least to him.

Her focus was their two daughters, her bridge and garden clubs, and the furnishings for the house they'd built on Loon Lake.

When it came to their daughters, she doted on their oldest, Mallory, who was willing to wear the clothing her mother chose and be dutiful in other ways. But Erin, their second and a tomboy who loved to join her dad in the fishing boat? Mary Lee finally gave up on trying to change her and just ignored the kid—which worked great for Erin. It was Mallory who would need years of therapy to recover from Mary Lee's dictatorial mothering.

Mary Lee's final frustration with Osborne had ended in an ironic twist. "Paul," she had insisted, "I demand you file a complaint with the county board to make Ray Pradt move that disgusting trailer of his. I can barely stand the sight of it every time I pull into our driveway." Of course Doc had never made the complaint.

Then it had been Ray Pradt who risked his own life when Osborne's car stalled, volunteering to drive his pickup through a dangerous blizzard to transport the woman who

despised him to the emergency room the last night of
her life.

* * *

The memories prompted by the mention of Jane Willoughby reminded Osborne of how fortunate he was to
have met Lewellyn Ferris, a woman who was not disappointed in him even when he cast his trout fly into the
branches of a tag alder—and who chuckled at his attempts
at humor. A woman who was a close friend *and* a lover.

Chapter Six

~

Scrambling to keep up with her mother, Katherine hurried up the steps to the lawyer's office, which was on the second floor of the bank building. She knew better than to ask Jane to slow down; she had learned years ago that when the woman was resolute, there was no stopping her. And this morning Jane Willoughby was the most resolute Katherine had ever seen her.

Without knocking, Jane pushed open the door to Robert Portman's office and rushed in, startling the woman seated at the desk in the front office. "Excuse me," said the woman, getting up out of her chair, "do you have an appointment?"

"No, I do not," said Jane, parking herself in the center of the room. Katherine sneaked in behind her. "Where's Rob?" Jane demanded.

"Right here," said a male voice from a doorway off to the right. "Jane. I wasn't expecting you . . ."

The look on Jane Willoughby's face stopped him. "What's wrong? Jane? Katherine? Are you ladies . . . is everyone okay?"

"No, I'm not." Jane moved toward the man in the doorway, her bulk forcing him to back into his office.

Catching the lawyer's eye as she followed her mother, Katherine raised her eyebrows to signal she had no idea what was coming next. The woman at the front desk continued to stare openmouthed at the three of them.

Leaning to one side in order to look past Jane, Rob Portman said to his secretary, "I have half an hour until my next client, don't I?"

"I'll give them a call right now and let them know you're running late," said the woman at the desk as he shut the door behind him.

"Bert's dead. Someone shot him this morning. Right now that's all I know," Jane announced, commandeering one of two chairs in front of his desk. "What I want from you is how our will reads so I know how much money I have—or don't have. Bert has never told me a damn thing about our finances, but I know he inherited a gazillion dollars from his old man and now I get everything. How much is it?"

Shock showed on the man's face, followed by consternation and discomfort. "Um, Jane," he hedged, nervous hands pushing at papers on his desk. "I am so sorry to hear—"

"I know, I know." Jane waved her hands as if to say *save it for the funeral*. "Just a ballpark figure, Rob. I've been waiting forty years for this."

"Mom," said Katherine, surprise in her voice, "are you serious? You and Dad never talked about money?"

"No we did not. It was a rule he made when we got married. My parents never talked money either. I know a woman wouldn't do that today, Katherine, but your dad was old-fashioned, and"—she shrugged—"I guess I was too."

"Jane, this is really not the time to be talking money—"

"I knew you'd say that, Rob. But I don't care what you think. Now answer my question—how much is our family worth?"

"Well, Jane, I'm really sorry to be the person to tell you this . . ." Rob sat so upright in his chair behind his desk that Katherine half expected him to levitate. "I guess . . . um . . . Bert didn't tell you that he filed for divorce, like, last Friday?" The man's voice squeaked. "You're to be served papers . . ."

"What the hell are you talking about?" Jane rose from her chair to lean over the desk toward him. "There's no divorce—*I'm his widow.*"

Rob looked so stricken that Katherine decided to jump in. "Mr. Portman, are you trying to say that my father filed for divorce?"

"Yes."

"Bullshit." Jane plunked her butt back in her chair. "That was Bert just being an idiot. He said crap like that all the time."

* * *

That part was true, thought Katherine. She had grown up hearing her parents screaming at each other, threatening to walk out, threatening to divorce. As a young child, she had found their fights terrifying. As a teenager, she had taken the battles as a signal she was free to escape the house.

"Mom, do you mind if we hear what Mr. Portman has to say?"

Jane grunted, but she kept quiet.

"All right, so . . ." said the lawyer, having moved a file out from under the stack on his desk.

As he started to read from the documents in front of him, Katherine kept her fingers crossed.

It had been over a year since she'd had discussions with her father about taking over his dental practice when he retired— just as he had taken over from his father—and she'd assumed that plan was in place. It was a guarantee of permanent employment; more important, running the practice would guarantee her a lifelong generous income, and she would be in charge. Had that changed? Had her father lied to her? She wanted to put both hands over her ears to shut out the lawyer's drone, but she knew better. Instead, she sat silent, listening.

"Bert's most significant assets are in that trust he inherited before your marriage, Jane. Over the years he has been careful to use only those monies when he purchased—"

Jane Willoughby interrupted him. "What you're really saying is he hid our money—all the money he's been making all these years on those stupid buildings and on his stocks. He hid his profits in that damn trust. That's what you're saying, isn't it?"

The lawyer shrugged and said, "You will be able to appeal this, Jane, but you may want to let me finish."

"Mom. Let's hear him out," said Katherine. "Remember, Dad may have *filed* for divorce, but a judge hasn't granted a divorce, so you are his widow."

"What the hell do you know?" Jane said, turning to Katherine and spitting her words out.

"I know that filing for divorce is not the same as a divorce being granted." Katherine hated to hear herself cowering. *God, I hate my mother*, she thought, gritting her teeth.

Jane turned her attention back to the lawyer. "Is my daughter right about that?"

"Yes, of course. You are officially, legally, the widow."

Katherine reached over to rub her mother's shoulders, but Jane pushed her hand away.

"A few details you should both be aware of," said Rob in a voice so level Katherine could see that he was anticipating another outburst. "Dr. Willoughby completed the sale of his practice two weeks ago." Rob gave Katherine a sympathetic look. "But the terms of the sale include the condition that the dentist purchasing his practice employ you, Katherine, for a minimum of ten years. The first two years will be at your current salary, after which that sum is to be increased ten percent every two years unless you choose to leave or renegotiate your annual salary."

When he saw Katherine's shocked expression, Rob spoke again, his tone gentle. "I thought you knew about this. No? I am so sorry. But that sale is complete, and there are now new owners."

Now it was Katherine's turn to be speechless. *How did I have no clue?* Oh, wait, now she remembered. Those two men she had seen walking through the office with Bert's assistant, Robin. Katherine had assumed they were reviewing the insurance policies for the practice. But they must have been representing the buyer . . .

"The good news—" Rob was saying.

"If there is any," said Jane, interrupting.

Rob ignored her. "The good news," he repeated, "is that there is a family estate of three-quarter of a million dollars, which is what he left to you, Jane. This is money earned after your marriage and separate from the assets Bert inherited from his father."

"So what happens to the rest?" Jane demanded. "What about his goddamn inheritance where he hid every penny he stole from me? And how much is that?"

"Roughly, the trust Bert inherited is currently worth five and a half million dollars. Bert's will states that those assets go to his . . . um, Robin—"

"That's it." Jane slammed a fist on the table. "I knew it! That goddamn Robin—" Jane was out of her chair, out the door, and out of the office before anyone could get a word in.

Katherine sat with her mouth open. She looked back at the lawyer. "Are you saying he left all that money to Robin—to Robin Steadman?" Katherine couldn't believe it. That kind, sweet, long-suffering dental assistant?

"God, no. Robin *Carpenter*, his pickleball partner. She is the woman who inherits the entire trust. You and your mother inherit the family estate, though he does leave the dental assistant five thousand dollars and the same amount to the Northwoods Pickleball Foundation."

Katherine at last found her voice. "And my dad's inheritance trust includes the sale of the practice?"

"Yes—and the house in Jackson Hole and that remarkable gun collection of Bert's. He bought those with the money he had inherited, and he sheltered them in that trust." Rob raised an index finger to underscore what he was about to say. "But Bert did add one mitigating factor, and it's in your favor, Katherine. While Robin Carpenter inherits the trust, if she remarries, then that trust goes to your mother—if she is still alive—and to you and your heirs. In that event, you and your mother would share the trust. The trust would also revert to you if Robin Carpenter were to die. Your father knew she is a Pecore, and he did not want that family getting what would be rightfully yours."

When Katherine didn't respond, he said, "Let me clarify: when Robin Carpenter remarries or dies, that trust reverts to the Willoughby family."

"I just don't understand how someone does this to . . . family." Katherine pushed back tears.

"Bert told me that Miss Carpenter is—was—the love of his life. He wanted her to know how special she was to him. His plan was for them to enjoy his retirement, to live like millionaires, to travel, and"—Rob's eyebrows lifted—"play pickleball."

"I see." Katherine sat silent for a long moment before speaking. "My father is dead, Rob. Did he sign that will?"

"Yes, he signed the will. That stands, I'm afraid. Your mother can contest it, but that would be complicated and quite expensive. As it stands, the two of you will receive three-quarters of a million dollars." He looked at her as he said with emphasis, "You will be *quite* comfortable."

Katherine stared back at him as she said, "You've been my father's lawyer for years. Right?"

Rob nodded.

"Did he ever try to divorce my mother before this?"

"Um, no . . ."

"But there were other women?"

"Katherine, I was your father's lawyer, not his close friend, so I don't know. And if I did know, I couldn't say."

The tone in Rob's voice and a barely discernible lift of his eyebrows told Katherine that there had indeed been other women. He didn't have to say so out loud—she got the message.

"But what I can say," Rob said, "is that I have no idea what made this woman so special." He offered a weak smile.

"Maybe she made him look good on the pickleball court?"

All she got from Rob Portman was a sad shrug.

* * *

Half an hour later, Katherine tried explaining the details to her mother. "Mom," she said, "the woman getting everything isn't Robin—"

"Shut up! I don't want to hear that name again."

Katherine knew Jane had the two Robins mixed up. She'd have to wait until her mother was in a better mood to explain.

Chapter Seven

❧

It was late morning, and Lew caught glimpses of the September sun beyond the still-green leaves of the maples guarding the old tennis court. Standing with Bruce, they were watching Robin Carpenter pace off where she had been standing on the pickleball court when Bert was shot.

His body had been transported by ambulance to the morgue at St. Mary's Hospital, but the chalk marks Lew had put down earlier stood out. Bruce had moved the crime scene tape to cordon off a larger area, saying, "In case we find any sign of a shooter closer to the victim. Sheriff Ferris, my people and I are well-trained investigators, but your buddy, Ray Pradt, has a sixth sense when it comes to tracking through the woods up here. Any chance you've got the budget for us to ask him to give this area the once-over? This old place is so overgrown and the brush around here so dense—he might see something we miss."

"Already texted him," said Lew. "Be here any minute."

"Hey, hear that?" said Robin Carpenter, pausing to raise one hand as they could hear a series of distant pops. "I told Sheriff Ferris that is exactly what I heard before Bert fell."

"You're hearing the Loon Lake Rifle Range," said Bruce, "I know the place. Passed it on the way out here." He turned and walked toward the dirt road running outside the fence bordering the tennis courts. Once on the road, he stopped to look down the slope to the shoreline below and gazed west across the lake to the distant shore. "Pretty far away. Not likely a bullet from there would have the momentum to do the kind of damage that would kill a man."

Seeing the question in Robin's eyes, Lew said, "Bruce is aware I found no exit wound on Dr. Willoughby's body, so we're sending it down to the Wausau Crime Lab for an official autopsy."

"If we're lucky, and I hope we are," said Bruce, "we'll recover the bullet in good condition. That's assuming it didn't fracture the skull, which could damage it. Hard to run ballistics on a damaged bullet."

Lew gave Bruce a quick look, signaling he might be sharing too much information around the traumatized woman who had, after all, seen the man she planned to marry die in front of her. At the sound of Bruce's words, Robin's hands had begun to tremble and she appeared close to tears.

"I have to think some idiot wasn't careful sighting their deer rifle this morning," said Lew.

"You sound like you want this to be an accident," said Bruce.

"I do. The thought of one person trying to kill another person? It's awful. It's why I do this job," said Lew, crossing her arms and rocking back on her heels. "To keep that from happening."

Bruce nodded, saying nothing. He turned to Robin and said, "I'm sure Sheriff Ferris has asked you this, but I— well, who do you think might want to, um, *hurt* Dr. Willoughby?"

"I can't imagine anyone," said Robin, tears now slipping down her cheeks. "I can't," she said, taking a deep breath and choking back a sob. "Bert is just the best. Everyone I know adores him, and he did so much for our pickleball club. He even paid for all new courts up at the high school . . ." She paused, shaking her head with her eyes closed. Bruce waited, silent. "But . . . I guess I can think of one guy who was pretty upset the other day . . ."

"The one who lives next door to this old place and has been so angry about the noise?" asked Lew. "I checked, and he has filed several complaints with the county board. I'll be talking to him this afternoon."

"No, this is a man who got hit hard by one of Bert's balls," said Robin. "He's on a team from Madison that we played two weeks ago. I know Bert didn't mean to, but he slammed a ball into the poor man's groin, and I know he was in a lot of pain. He dropped out of the tournament right after he got hit."

"But pickleballs are so light," said Bruce.

"Not when a man as big as Bert Willoughby puts all his weight behind it," said a voice from behind Lew.

"Hey, Doc, how are you?" said Bruce, turning to look past the fence to where Osborne was walking toward them on the dirt road.

"That's your place right down the road, isn't it, Doc? I thought it looked familiar," said Bruce.

"Yep, I'm maybe a quarter mile up the road. This is quite a place, isn't it?" said Osborne as he walked toward them. He gave a wave in the direction of the boarded-up buildings and the grounds surrounding the tennis court. "When I was growing up, this was *the* place for Chicagoans to send their boys for the summer," he said. "My dad was the dentist for the camp and its owners, so I spent my summers running all around here."

"Why hasn't someone bought it?" asked Bruce. "Right on the lake like this? Could be a great summer home."

"Bert Willoughby bought a section of it," said Osborne, pointing. "This area with the old tennis court and down that way where there used to be a baseball field. The problem with the property is that the lodge is built too far from the shoreline, so you don't get good views. Add to that the cost to put in a new well and septic and gas—that has to be astronomical."

"Not to mention fiber optics," said Bruce with an understanding nod.

As the two men chatted, Lew put a hand on Osborne's arm and gave a jerk of her head to let him know someone had arrived.

The four of them turned to see an SUV that had just pulled up and watched as a woman got out. She was quite tall and broad shouldered, with short, straight, light-brown hair worn pushed back from a square-shaped full face. Watching her advance toward them, Osborne thought, as he always did, that seldom had he seen anyone look so similar to a parent as Katherine Willoughby did to her father. There wasn't a hint of Jane in their daughter's appearance.

"Dr. Willoughby," said Osborne, stepping forward. "Katherine, I am so sorry to hear what has happened." He gestured toward Lew and Bruce. "I'm sure you know Sheriff Ferris, and this is Bruce Peters with the Wausau Crime Lab." He turned to them, saying, "I'd like you to meet Dr. Willoughby's daughter, Dr. Katherine Willoughby. Dr. Willoughby joined her father's practice recently."

Then he paused to look at Robin. "I'm sorry, we haven't met. I'm Dr. Paul Osborne, and you are?"

"Robin Carpenter," said Robin. "I'm Bert's pickleball partner." She gave a frightened glance in Katherine's direction.

"I'm afraid I have to ask you to stay back," said Lew with a wave toward Katherine. "This is still a crime scene until we can confirm the cause of your father's death."

"Excuse me, Sheriff Ferris," said Robin with an anxious look on her face. "I need to get going, but I have a question for Mr. Peters." She turned toward Bruce and asked, "My pickleball team likes to use this practice court, but will that be impossible now? I was hoping that tomorrow . . ."

"No, I'm sorry. Our techs will be working here for several days. I'm afraid you'll have to find somewhere else to practice."

Worry crossed Robin's face. She looked around hesi-
tantly, then pointed to the far end of the courts. "Would
over there be okay? The old surface is cracked, but we don't
need a lot of space, and we can sweep up the leaves and
stuff. If we set up our net in the far corner, would that
be okay?"

Bruce looked around him and then off in the direction
of the fourth court before nodding and saying, "Sure, that's
far enough away from this area. But please make sure no
one gets near this area. Don't come chasing a ball, for
instance. It'll be cordoned off, but I cannot emphasize
enough that no one should even walk *near*—"

"Oh, gosh, no. I'll make sure everyone is very, very careful. And we practice quite early—like six thirty in the
morning. Several on my team have jobs. We'll be done by
eight at the latest."

"Then that should be fine," said Bruce. He turned to the
woman who had walked up and was standing nearby with
an impatient expression on her face. "Yes, Dr. Willoughby,
how can I help you?"

"I want to see where my father died." Her voice was
hard. Even as she spoke to Bruce, she continued to stare at
Robin Carpenter. The stare was too much. Robin turned
away and started off toward her car.

"No, wait, Ms. Carpenter, please," said Bruce, "I may
have a few more questions." Robin stopped and stood silent,
her eyes on the ground.

"Over there, Katherine," said Lew, pointing at the
chalked diagram on the asphalt and hoping to defuse the

moment. "The net has been taken down, but it was here that your dad was practicing for a pickleball tournament."

"Right. *Pickleball*," said Katherine, never lifting her eyes from Robin and managing to make pickleball sound like a lewd pastime rather than a sport.

With those words, she turned, strode back to her car, got in, and drove off. Watching her go, no one said a word. Bruce motioned to Robin and asked her to show him exactly where she had been standing and moving while practicing.

* * *

Walking into her parents' home twenty minutes later, Katherine found Jane on the phone.

"Oh, damn." Jane slammed the phone down. "Can't even get a funeral planned. The woman at that stupid sheriff's office said I can't bury Bert until sometime next week *at the earliest*." The words came out in the shriek Katherine's mother used whenever people didn't do what she demanded.

"Mom, they're trying to find out—"

"Don't tell me! I know what they're doing." With that, Jane strode off to the kitchen, leaving Katherine standing in the front hall. She knew it was useless to try to placate the woman.

At the sound of a soft knock on the front door, Katherine reached back to open the door. Robin Steadman stood there. She was holding a rifle against her right shoulder, the barrel pointing back and up.

"Not loaded," she said, seeing the surprise in Katherine's eyes. Standing in one spot, she dropped her head slightly as she managed to whisper, "I am so sorry, Dr. Willoughby. Patients are very upset. They want to know if there's anything anyone can do . . ."

"Who knows," Katherine said with a shrug. "Won't you come in, Robin? Have a cup of coffee?"

"No, I won't stay. Bert loaned me this." She held out the rifle. "I had a weasel going after my chickens in the coop on my farm. This took care of it. Thought I'd put it back, if that's okay with you. Bert is particular how he keeps his guns organized, you know."

Katherine was stunned to hear Robin refer to her father by his first name. So they were more than boss and subordinate? They were friends? Robin always addressed him formally in the office, but obviously she was comfortable using his first name otherwise. *Interesting.* Was Robin Steadman one of the "other women" that Rob Portman's lifted eyebrows had implied? Had there been a once-upon-a-time intimate relationship between those two? Robin had worked for Bert for over ten years, and she was in her thirties. Nor was she unattractive. *Could be . . .*

Coming back to the moment, Katherine glanced over her shoulder, hoping Jane wouldn't walk up. "Sure, come in. Dad rarely let me touch those, so I have no idea—"

"This is a nice Browning AR, but it isn't one of his treasures," said Robin, walking into the gun room. "It's the workhorse that he saved for us to use with critters like rabbits and beavers and my weasel." She set the gun onto a rack at one end of the far wall and stepped back.

"Yeah, I know," said Katherine. "It's the only one he ever let me use."

Robin looked over at Katherine and said, "I went ahead and canceled all his appointments. With your permission, I'll encourage people to see Dr. Carey when he takes over, if that's okay? I believe that was the agreement he had with your father."

"That makes sense, but . . ." Katherine hesitated. "How long have you known about the sale of the practice?"

"Oh, heavens, at least six months, I guess. Your dad talked to me right away. He wanted my opinion on Dr. Carey since he's fresh out of dental school and—"

"Right," said Katherine, interrupting her. She couldn't bear to hear more. Impossible to believe how her dad had betrayed her.

"Out! Out of my house!" Jane's screeching caught Katherine by surprise. She had walked into the hall and was heading toward them, waving her arms at Robin. Robin, looking stunned, stammered something, but Katherine grabbed her by the arm and walked her quickly to the door.

"It's okay, Robin. Mom is quite upset with everyone. As you can imagine. I'll be back in the office tomorrow morning, okay?"

Katherine turned to her mother and was ready to explode herself when Deb Wallace, the woman who cleaned house for her parents, came walking down the hall toward them. "Calm down, Mom," said Katherine in a firm tone. She turned to the slim, light-haired woman who was carrying a laundry basket and appeared to have a question.

"With Dr. Willoughby not here to care for those guns that aren't in cabinets, would you like me to keep them dusted?" asked Deb.

"Don't touch the damn things," commanded Jane, and she flounced off to the small room down the hall that she used as her office.

"Dr. Willoughby? Is that all right with you?" asked Deb, after Jane had disappeared. "I will be cleaning in the room anyway—vacuuming and such. It's not a problem."

"For right now, let's just leave it," said Katherine. Deb walked off, and Katherine took a chair in the living room. She needed time to think.

No, she had never been close with her father. The idea that he had been so friendly with Robin Steadman? A woman not that much older than her? A woman in the same field but without her professional credentials? That was irritating. *No*, thought Katherine, *it's* upsetting *is what it is.*

Chapter Eight

"Lunchtime and no sign of Ray," said Lew, sounding mystified and feeling hungry as she walked over to where Bruce was standing with two of his colleagues. Osborne had already left to walk back to his place. Meanwhile, Bruce and the others had managed to push the curious bystanders back beyond the dirt road surrounding the boys' camp while Lew promised the television and newspaper reporters she would hold a press conference late that afternoon.

"Lunchtime and I'm ready for a break," said Bruce with a chuckle as he picked up on her words. "Think Ray's got anything besides walleyes in his fridge?"

"He better have a good excuse for not showing up here," said Lew. "I texted him over an hour ago. Come on, let's see what that razzbonya's up to."

"Don't twist my arm," said Bruce with a bounce of his eyebrows that meant he was happy.

Minutes later Lew pulled her cruiser into the clearing in front of the giant neon-green muskie that doubled as the trailer home for the man who managed to make a life on the water pay off better than anything a college degree could promise.

"Jeez," said Bruce, staring at the huge fake fish as Lew turned off the ignition. "How do you make something like that?"

"You promise a talented carpenter a decade of bluegills delivered weekly," said Lew in a grim tone. "No, I have no idea. Ray knows weird people."

Bruce hadn't even closed the door on the passenger side of Lew's cruiser when he said, "I smell something wonderful . . . and it's not liver sausage."

"Sorry, Lew," said Ray, walking out his screen door, still wearing a flour-covered apron. "I had five apple pies to get in the oven when you texted. So I'm very sorry, and please don't tell me someone died because of me." His tone was light, but the worry in his eyes was genuine.

"No one died because of you . . . yet. But Bruce and I do have a serious problem, and we need your help—"

"How long till the first one is out?" asked Bruce, interrupting her as he walked toward Ray.

"Maybe fifteen minutes."

"So I'm smelling pie, huh? Got any Nueske's liver sausage?"

Lew rolled her eyes in defeat. Bruce was relentless.

"Yep, and rye bread and Dijon mustard." Relief crossed Ray's face. Lew knew he'd be up at the camp tennis courts once she and Bruce had had their lunch. "But first, you gotta tell me," said Ray, perking up, "what did the one lake say to the other lake?"

Bruce shrugged. "You got me."

"Nothing. They just waved. Okay, now you can enter." Ray stepped back to hold the screen door open. "After you, good friends."

"Oh no, wait." Bruce stopped so fast that Lew bumped into him. "What the hell?"

Lew peered past Bruce's shoulder. "Oh, oh," she said, "a crawler convention? Are we interrupting an important meeting?"

"Ohmygod, did those go into the pies?" Bruce pointed at a cluster of night crawlers writhing on Ray's kitchen table. Nearby was a cutting board covered with a tangle of line and clumps of fish hooks.

"Of course," said Ray. He turned to Lew with a sheepish look. "I did have to finish the pies, but I also had to make sure I had a couple good worm harnesses ready for my podcast tonight. Please tell me I haven't really screwed things up?"

"No, but don't ask me for a raise." She punched him in the arm. She knew Ray's podcast on all things muskie fishing was so successful, especially with sporting goods advertisers, that he was making serious money—so much that he no longer had to help out at the cemetery digging graves when short of cash.

Fact was, not only was Ray the most talented tracker in the Northwoods, but he had come through so often, working twenty-four hour stretches when needed, that Lew had complete confidence in his talent and in his work ethic. She knew that once she got him out of the kitchen, she could count on a thorough search of the entire campgrounds.

Doc Osborne's coffee crowd had once said of Ray Pradt that "he could track a snake over a rock." He could and he would, and she knew that.

"Bert Willoughby was shot playing pickleball up at the old boys' camp," said Lew. "Happened a few hours ago. You must have heard the sirens."

"I did but figured it was just some tourist capsized their kayak. So you need me to find the bullet and—"

"No, there's no exit wound, and I've sent the body down to the Wausau Crime Lab for an autopsy. Pretty sure they'll recover the bullet that killed Willoughby. I could be wrong," said Lew, "but I think someone may have shot him accidentally—like sighting their deer rifle and not paying attention to the direction they were shooting. Might have got antsy waiting for a spot at the rifle range and went out to the parking lot to shoot. It's happened before."

"I have two of my investigators scouring the immediate area around those old tennis courts in case someone has made it a practice to shoot in that direction," said Bruce. "No sign of more bullets so far."

"So you need me to check the grounds beyond the lodge and the tennis courts?"

"Yes," said Lew. "As soon as your pies are done, please."

"Good idea," said Ray. "Someone shot Bert Willoughby? Excuse me, but I can think of a half dozen guys would love to see that guy dead. Me included."

"You're exaggerating," said Lew.

"I am, but . . . you take a guy as stingy and mean-spirited as that old dentist, and who knows?"

"Stingy? I thought the Willoughbys were well-to-do. They certainly have a lovely home. What are you talking about?" asked Lew.

"Nickel-and-dime stuff," said Ray. "Like when I had just started my guiding business, Bert hired me for a day. He's not good at taking advice, so he ignored pretty much everything I suggested and ended up with one muskie too small to keep. Refused to pay me. Said I was a lousy guide and walked away." He shook his head. "That does not win you friends. That plus my old man said he's a lousy dentist to boot. He had a couple patients he thought should have sued the guy for malpractice."

"Ray's father is a retired doctor," said Lew, explaining Ray's comment to Bruce. "But nice guy or not, Bert Willoughby didn't deserve a bullet in the head. Bruce and I have our jobs to do, and I need your help."

"Hey, Lew," said Bruce, who had walked into the kitchen and was standing near the stove. "He didn't tell a complete lie. I'm looking at two pies cooling here."

"Two more in the oven and one last one to go when those come out," said Ray. "They bake for a half hour only. Then I put 'em in the freezer until I want one and finish baking it then. That way I can have fresh apple pie all winter. So, yeah, in half an hour is when I was going to catch up with you two. Lew didn't say it was an emergency."

"It is and it isn't," said Lew. "Can we move the worms before we eat?"

"What on earth is a worm harness?" asked Bruce, walking back toward the table. "Something for a worm race?"

"Now there's an idea," said Ray with a chuckle. "Actually it's a bait rig that I make with leader lines, beads, and hooks to use for trolling. The worm harness has two lines—one works to keep the night crawler close to the bottom, where the fish are, while the other line helps to keep it from snagging on anything. I'm teaching how to make the darn things on my podcast tonight, because right now—early September—is the best time of year for muskie fishing, especially around sunken logs and boulders. I want my fans well prepared."

"Your fans?" asked Bruce.

"Yep, I got six hundred fifty-four thousand and twelve people who listen every week."

"I see," said Bruce as he covered his rye bread with slices of liver sausage. "That's a lot of listeners. I'm impressed," he said with his mouth full.

"God forbid you help me catch a killer and let 'em down," said Lew, reaching for the Dijon mustard. "Just kidding." She grinned.

Three sandwiches, one worm harness, and three slices of pie later, lunch was over. Lew tossed her paper napkin into the kitchen trash can and asked, "Ray, are you familiar with Bert Willoughby's daughter, Katherine? Wouldn't she be about your age?"

"Oh yes," said Ray as he gathered up their lunch plates. "When we were in first grade together at St. Mary's, she decided I should marry her."

"That had to be fun," said Bruce. "She seems rather intimidating. My impression, anyway. Must have taken all your six-year-old skills to avoid the altar."

"So that's where you got your early training," said Lew, winking at Bruce.

Ray was famous for attracting women only to leave them disappointed when they learned the hard way he wasn't lying when he said he was a confirmed bachelor. At least that's how Ray's life had gone so far. But at age thirty-two, Lew thought, of course he had years ahead to reconsider.

"That experience wasn't as funny as it sounds," said Ray. "I turned her proposal down, and next thing my mom gets a call from the school principal. She had to meet with Jane Willoughby, Katherine's mother, who said I had been rude and broke her daughter's heart. When my mom heard the whole story—how Katherine thought I should be her sweetheart and apologize—my mom stood up and walked out of the meeting. She moved me from St. Mary's to the other grade school. So the Willoughbys have never been family friends."

"She certainly doesn't like pickleball players," said Bruce pointedly.

"She gave that woman who was Bert's partner the dim eye, didn't she?" said Lew, agreeing. "Rather rude, in my opinion."

"That's the family," said Ray. "That's what they're like. But Bert Willoughby has run a successful dental practice and some folks love him, I'm sure."

*   *   *

After letting herself out through the screen door, Lew decided to walk down to the shoreline and out onto Ray's dock. "This afternoon sun is too beautiful to miss," she said over her shoulder to Bruce, who had followed behind her.

At the end of the dock, she paused to look out over the lake. Shards of sunlight had shattered the solid bank of pale gray that had been hovering overhead. Now fluffy clouds glowed white against an azure sky as they simultaneously ignited the still surface of the lake: a universe of sun, sky, and cloud. Not even the sound of a distant motorboat marred the moment.

I live in a beautiful place, thought Lew as she turned to walk back to her cruiser. Bruce nodded and followed in silence. Both knew better than to let words spoil the silent glory.

"We'll fish tonight," said Lew as she dropped him off at the camp. "Pick you up around five unless another numb-nut sights their rifle carelessly."

"So you do think it's just an accident," said Bruce.

"Don't you?"

"I need to know more—and we will soon. See you at five."

* * *

Lew hadn't been at her desk two minutes when Dani walked in, holding her laptop open. "Sheriff Ferris, you won't believe it, but we've had seven anonymous tips phoned in from people who are *certain* they know who shot Dr. Willoughby."

"Seven?" Lew was taken aback.

"Yes. Five are women, and I know who they are." Dani gave a proud smile.

"You do? By tracing the phone numbers?"

"Nope. I recognize their voices from the salon."

Dani was the IT expert for the McBride County Sheriff's Department, but it wasn't because she had majored in computer science. No, she had been focused on styling hair when, by accident, Lew had recognized her natural talent for IT work.

It happened during an investigation Lew was involved in at the local community college where Dani was majoring in cosmetology. After Dani volunteered to search the office computers, she did so with such speed and accuracy that Lew recognized that the young woman had an aptitude similar to that of a pianist who plays by ear.

Soon Lew had convinced her to follow a career path that might be more lucrative than styling hair and makeup. But Dani loved being a beautician and still worked weekends at her best friend's hair salon. Lew thought that was fine, and possibly even a boon to the sheriff's department. Dani heard women tell all when seated in their hairdresser's chair. All and more. One never knew when that might come in handy.

"So you're sure about these?" asked Lew, glancing over the names and comments on Dani's screen.

"Not a hundred percent," said Dani, "but it's a start."

Chapter Nine

～

It was nearly six when Lew pulled the old pickup she used for fishing into the clearing at the Prairie River. She was an hour later than planned. When questions from the reporters ran longer than she had expected, she'd called Osborne and asked him to pick Bruce up at the Loon Lake Lodge. She was surprised they hadn't already arrived.

Reaching into the back of her truck for her rod case and waders, she made a mental note to try to arrange a trip north to the Elvoy, a trout stream located just over the border into Michigan. Even though she had been stalked by a black bear determined to guard the riverbank on her last trip up there, she knew the trout were too smart for that old guy. Bruce would love the Elvoy: bear, trout, and all.

Doc's SUV pulled up just as she was tying her boots. She looked up in time to see Bruce leap from the passenger seat, his fishing duffel already open. "Sorry to be late, Lew," he said, bustling down to a flat rock under the tag alders, where he plunked himself down and opened his duffel. "My fault, not Doc's."

He yanked his waders out of his duffel and went on. "Got a call from the pathologist who did the autopsy on your victim. He got the bullet, and the good news is that it didn't hit bone, so no damage. Should be an easy one for the ballistics analysis once we have the gun." By the time Bruce finished talking, he had his waders half on and was stumbling over the rock-strewn riverbank, anxious to follow Lew into the trout stream.

Glancing up past the pines protecting the stream, she could see streaks of fuchsia in the soft clouds overhead, a sign the sun was likely to set by seven thirty. *Drat*, thought Lew. The days were shortening—the only drawback to September fishing.

Doc was less frantic than his companions. Seated on a large boulder, he pulled on his waders while listening to Lew and Bruce chat as they waded into the water. He watched Lew stop to observe Bruce's first casts. She had been teaching him the double haul, which she had also been teaching Osborne. But while Bruce was improving, his casting smoother, Osborne was still struggling with the motions. Breaking habits he'd picked up over years of fishing for muskie and walleye with a spinning rod was not easy. And so he studied the younger man's moves and listened to his instructor, hoping to hear a magic word or two of advice that might help him.

"Good . . . good . . . keep your hauling arm flexed . . . yes . . . good try. Once more," said Lew, and Osborne could see Bruce set his jaw as he moved both arms to execute a cast. "Stop, Bruce," said Lew, her voice critical and crisp.

"Think of your line hand moving in a recoil kind of motion . . . yes! That was perfect. Trust your *feel* of the rod instead of thinking so hard. Bruce . . . yes! See what I mean? You did it! That cast was so smooth it had to feel like dancing. Right?"

Bruce's happy eyebrows said it all.

Ah, dancing, thought Osborne. *I'll try that. I've always been a good dancer. Maybe, if I think* dancing, *that'll help my casting.* He reached for his rod case. Unlike Bruce, who seemed to live life in a rush, he liked to take his time, especially when getting ready to fish. "Go slow and make every move count," his father had said years ago. Osborne liked that advice and did his best to stick to it.

Once Bruce had made three successful double hauls, Lew led the way upstream. When she reached a favorite spot, she stopped. Leaning over, she studied the streambed for a long couple of minutes before reaching for her fly case. After scrutinizing the contents, she made a choice, tucked the case back in her vest pocket, and began to tie on a small nymph trout fly.

"What on earth is that?" asked Bruce, who had paused his casting to watch her.

"Oh, something I haven't tried in ages," she said. "Just the other day I was reading about nymph fishing with a size-twenty Micro Perdigon Ginger UV. I've had one for years and I thought I'd try it, since I see we have a lot of mayfly larvae tonight. If there's one thing I know, it's that brookies love larvae and the nymph trout fly simulates the larval stage of the mayfly. This one that I'm tying on is small, but it has a weighted bead that'll get it through the surface and down close to the streambed. We'll see what happens next. I don't have the right leader, so it might not work. Fun to try, though."

Bruce shook his head. "Too technical for me. I'm gonna keep dancing."

* * *

An hour later, he and Osborne stepped out of the Prairie and sat down to munch on trail mix that Bruce had brought along. "I won't be having any dinner until after eight," he said, reaching for another handful of nuts and raisins. "Hard to wait that long."

Lew, who was just upstream and around a bend, could hear them talking. A large tag alder whose branches extended out over the trout stream hid her from their sight. She was about to head their way when she heard Bruce say, "That Katherine woman who showed up at the tennis courts—do you know her? She struck me as rather . . . hmm . . ."

"Formidable?" asked Osborne.

"That's a good way to put it. I got the impression she was out to bully that poor pickleball player as if it was her fault that guy was shot."

"*Bully* is a family tradition in the Willoughby household," said Osborne with a chuckle. Intrigued by the two men's conversation, Lew decided to stay right where she was. Eavesdropping was not a bad research tool.

"The old man was a bully of the first order," said Osborne. "I've known that joker since I was a kid. He was one reason I was okay with my father sending me off to boarding school. We were in kindergarten together, and he was mean then."

"That's right, your mother died when you were quite young. How old were you, Doc?"

"Six. My poor dad had no family to step in and help us, so off I went to a Jesuit boarding school down in the southern part of the state. I was there through high school, which is why I love it up here in the Northwoods. For me, being here means vacation." The two men laughed.

"I guess that's okay if your wife likes it too."

"Oh, my late wife hated it." Osborne's tone turned serious. "Likely why she hated me too." A long silence ensued, and Lew was about to move downstream when she heard Osborne say, "That's what I like about Lewellyn. She loves being outdoors; she's as crazy about fishing as I am. On water, in water—doesn't matter. Just being outdoors makes her smile. And, Bruce, I love that woman's smile."

"I know what you mean," said Bruce. "That little grin of hers, those happy eyes. I am so lucky I latched on to her as my fly-fishing instructor. She makes me work, but, man, she makes it happen. Too bad about your wife. Guess she never knew what she was missing, huh?"

"She was never into anything outdoors. Dinner parties, bridge club, golf—you name it, that was her thing. We were so different. I like that young people today live together today before they get married; they get to know each other, you know?"

Again there was a silence between the two men. Lew waited.

"I wasn't surprised to see Katherine be so obnoxious this morning," said Osborne. "Reminds me of her mother, Jane. She's another one just like Bert: a bully." He paused for a moment and then went on. "Now that we're talking about those women, I remember listening to Mary Lee—that's my late wife—and Jane Willoughby plot to kick this one woman out of their bridge and garden clubs. They didn't know I was sitting in my den where I could hear every word. I heard them complain how the woman, Julia was her name, how they thought she was smiling too much at Bert, so they decided to ostracize her from their clubby little crowd. I'll tell you, those two women were something else: nice on the surface and pre-e-etty nasty underneath."

"Sounds like a few people I've known," said Bruce, munching another handful of nuts.

"Mean, just plain mean, is what they were. I heard from my daughter, Erin, who was friends with Julia's daughter, that her mom was devastated by the lies that Mary Lee and Jane spread. Thanks to those two, Julia and her family ended up moving away from Loon Lake."

"Yep, Jane Willoughby, like her husband, is something else. She reminds me of a pudgy wolf spider. Like the ones I find on the floor of my garage."

"That's an appealing image," said Bruce through his munching. "Got anything kind to say?" He laughed.

"I have to shut up," said Osborne with a chuckle. "I'm giving the poor wolf spider a bad rap. Oh well, now you've got me going, I have one more story about that family."

"Don't stop now, Doc. I'm enjoying this."

Lew was too.

"Years ago there was an incident with the daughter, Katherine, which I heard about because she was in the same class as Erin. Their high school class was voting for their prom court, and Katherine was elected queen. Erin and her friends were convinced there had been cheating, because Katherine wasn't well liked.

"But it wasn't until a month or two after the prom that one of the high school security guards was reviewing videos from the school's surveillance cameras and saw Katherine sneak into the principal's office and mess around with a pile of papers on one of the secretary's desks. The guard hunted with a friend of mine, said he checked the date on the video record, and it was the date of the voting for the prom court. No one did anything about it, but Erin and her friends knew."

"So Dr. Katherine Willoughby isn't above a little cheating?" asked Bruce.

"Like I said—family tradition."

"But, Doc," said Bruce, "given that Bert Willoughby had a few personality flaws, was he a good dentist? Is his daughter?"

"No idea about her. I sold my practice before she joined Bert's. Let me put it this way—Bert was a moneymaker. He did the minimum for what he charged, he took only patients who didn't have dental insurance so he could charge the maximum, and he stiffed plenty of his suppliers. I know the latter because of complaints I've heard over the years. And his cleanliness standards would make you throw up. That was until he hired Robin Steadman as his assistant. She cleaned the place up. That's what I was told by my staff at the time."

Osborne's voice rose as he went on. "Let me ask you this, Bruce. Do you want the health of your teeth, your mouth, and your upper digestive tract dependent on a guy who does everything on the cheap and refuses to wash his hands between patients?"

Bruce shook his head. "Why on earth did people go to him?"

"Beats me. But Bert Willoughby has always been a charmer—tall, good-looking, excellent athlete. And he and Jane put up a good front with their expensive house, expensive car, summer cottage on the most expensive lake. People don't think it through. They go to the doctor or dentist who looks good, sounds good, makes them feel good. Doesn't matter that he or she might be an incompetent idiot."

"Hey, Doc, don't hold back," said Bruce with a chuckle.

"I know, I know. Enough of that. Let's talk about something more pleasant," said Osborne. "Can I tell you what I like about Lewellyn Ferris besides her fishing?"

"Careful," said Bruce with a smile in his voice. "I may be too young to hear this . . ."

"She *listens*," said Osborne, emphasizing his last word. "She has a good *heart*. She's kind and she listens. You can't ask for more."

"I know what you mean," said Bruce. "That's my wife too. She isn't the prettiest girl in the room, but she sure as hell understands me and loves me just the same. Need some more trail mix?"

Lew saw him holding out the nearly empty bag as she came around the corner. "Any luck, you two?" she asked with a grin.

"Nope," said the men in unison.

"But we *talked* fishing," said Bruce. "Ready to head back to town?"

"I am," said Lew. "Long day ahead. Doc, I'll be at my place tonight. See you for coffee in the morning?"

"With a doughnut," said Osborne as he gave her a peck on the cheek.

Chapter Ten

At Jane's direction, Katherine picked up two chicken dinners to go from the deli section at the Loon Lake Market. It wasn't easy. Four people stopped her as she waited in line to pay, saying they had "heard the awful news." All of them added a variation of "You poor thing. Please give your mom a hug for me." Four people, four variations of the same message.

After nodding and mumbling "Thank you" at least four times, Katherine was able to extricate herself and head back to her parents' house. She figured it would help her mother if they ate together before Katherine left for the night. She had her own place, a cozy condo overlooking the Wisconsin River. The thought of a quiet evening after the tumult of the day, especially the session with her father's lawyer, kept her going.

* * *

"What? Where the hell do you think *you're* going?" asked Jane, demanding as ever, when she saw Katherine stand up from the kitchen table where they had eaten and reach into her purse for her car keys.

"What do you mean, where?" asked Katherine. "I'm just going home, Mom."

"And leaving me all alone on a terrible night like this?" It wasn't despair that Katherine saw in her mother's eyes—it was anger. A fight. *Oh god*, thought Katherine, deciding to give in before things got worse.

"Okay, Mom, don't worry. I'll stay here with you."

"Damn right you'll stay." Jane slammed down the fork she'd been using to eat the half-frozen Pepperidge Farm lemon cake that Katherine had brought with the chickens. "I've been through enough today without you messing things up."

"*Messing things up?*" Katherine sighed. "I just thought you might appreciate time alone."

"Oh, what do you know? I don't need *time alone*," said Jane, mimicking Katherine. "I need help. I need you to figure out how we cancel that damn will. God, Bert was stupid. What kind of idiot writes something like that? And that Robin? Coming to our house this morning? Who the hell does she think she is?"

Jane threw her paper napkin on the table and got to her feet just as Katherine was trying to say, "She's not the Robin that Dad put—" But Jane had stomped out of the kitchen. Katherine could hear her climbing the stairs to her bedroom.

"So you're staying here tonight," said Jane, calling down after she had reached the second-floor landing. It wasn't a question—it was an order.

* * *

Growing up the only child of Bert and Jane Willoughby, Katherine had never felt close to her parents. Her mother criticized everything, from how she walked ("Stand up straight, for God's sake") to what she wore ("You look awful in those pants—why do I spend a fortune on your clothes?"). The worst had been during her early teens, when she'd overheard Jane on the phone complaining to one of her women friends: "Katherine is getting way too tall, and her hair is awful—she's gonna end up looking like her father . . ."

Her father didn't help. Between his days in the dental office, weekends on the golf course, and weeknights spent glued to sports on the television in their living room, Bert wasn't around much. His exchanges with her when she was a growing girl had been simple: "Quiet, now. I'm trying to watch this."

And so she felt alone in their home. Yes, her mom took her shopping for clothes, but even that was agonizing, as Jane would pull out blouses and skirts and pants in sizes too small, then grunt as she had to go back for something two sizes larger.

On two occasions, Bert had reluctantly agreed to let her use one of his Browning rifles, but only because the high school wanted every student to take hunter safety classes— deer hunting was a given for anyone over twelve in the Northwoods. The high school reasoned that even if their students, male or female, didn't hunt themselves, they were sure to be around people with guns. He had made it clear that she was not to go near any of his other guns, telling her, "This is my dad's old rabbit rifle. You can't damage it, but don't you dare touch any of my good guns. Let's hope you can shoot better than your mother. She's hopeless."

One thing Katherine never understood was why her father wouldn't share any information about the gun collection that he obsessed over. Even after she proudly showed him a research report she had done on antique Brownings, he had refused to talk to her about his firearms. "Girls don't understand this stuff," he'd said.

She even signed up for lessons at the shooting range, hoping that might encourage her father to take her along to the gun shows or even out hunting when he joined his pals during season. But when she asked about going along during deer season, his response had been scathing: "Are you kidding, Kath?" He called her *Kath* when she irritated him. "Women aren't welcome at my deer shack."

He had, however, seemed flattered when she announced she was going to follow his footsteps into dentistry, although when she was home on vacation from dental school, she'd had to push him to show her his offices. That was how she'd met Robin Steadman.

Robin was standing nearby when Bert brushed off Katherine's request to know more about the practice. When he walked off to see a patient, Robin had offered to show her the small lab and explain the other office procedures, including recordkeeping and referrals to oral surgeons and pharmacies—all key to running a dental practice.

After graduating from the university's School of Dentistry, Katherine had joined a practice in Madison, thinking she could pick up good business practices there that she might apply to her father's practice, which she assumed she would take over when he retired. But two years later, when Katherine had suggested joining Bert's practice, the only person who listened to her was Robin Steadman.

That's when it became obvious to Katherine that it was Robin who made sure everything in the office ran smoothly; it was Robin Steadman who was in charge. When it came to Katherine's work, Bert remained oblivious to her long hours and expertise with patients. It was kind, gentle Robin Steadman who nodded approvals and who had the welcoming smile when she arrived every morning.

When Katherine was ready to move back to Loon Lake to join Bert's practice, she was determined to live at a distance from her parents, even though her mother invited her to share their six-bedroom home with its elegant winding oak staircase ("You can have the east wing and plenty of privacy, honey"). Katherine suspected the invitation was extended so her mother could brag to her women friends: "I thought she would love to join us in our lovely home, where she could have her own wing." But, wing or no wing, Katherine didn't need the criticism or the constant reminder that she was a nobody to either of them.

* * *

After Jane had flounced out of the kitchen, Katherine put away the dishes, threw out the Styrofoam containers their dinner had come in, and decided to go up to her childhood bedroom. She paused in the downstairs hall, looking into the darkened room where Bert's guns were on display. She thought of Robin and the well-used Browning rifle she had returned earlier that day.

Turning on the light switch, she walked over to the rack where the gun was kept—the gun that had belonged to her grandfather, the gun that was used to shoot rabbits. So her father had shared it with Robin, had he? The same one he had let his daughter use only three times: once for the hunter safety training, once for her lessons at the shooting range, and once for that father-daughter hunting day. This was interesting. Why share the gun so readily with his dental assistant? Again Katherine considered the question: Had he had an affair with Robin Steadman too?

Katherine turned and walked out of the room, turning off the light, and headed up to her bedroom.

Late that night she was awakened by the sound of her mother's feet padding down the stairs. Katherine waited, then stole to her bedroom door, opened it, and looked down the stairway. The light was on in the little room her mother called "my den." Katherine closed her door, climbed back into bed, and waited. After about fifteen minutes, she heard her mother come back up the stairs.

Katherine got out of bed again. This time she crept down the winding staircase, stopping to look into her mother's den. She saw what appeared to be two letters on the desk by her mother's purse. Katherine debated trying to see who her mother was writing but decided against it. She didn't need more anger.

Instead, she tiptoed into the gun room. She stared at the Browning AR that Robin Steadman had returned.

Robin had been holding the gun in her hands and was the last person to touch it.

Katherine opened the drawer below the gun rack where her father kept cartridges for the guns. She picked up the box holding the cartridges for the old Browning, but it turned out that it had been opened, and half a dozen cartridges clattered onto the floor. She stood still, listening. Had the sound of the cartridges hitting the wood floor awakened Jane? She waited . . . no sound.

Bending down, she gathered up the cartridges and slipped them back into the box, taking care not to drop them again. She set the box back in the drawer, closed it carefully, and turned to go back upstairs.

She couldn't go back to sleep. She found herself agonizing over the meeting with the lawyer. She couldn't believe Bert had sold the business. He was essentially pushing her out of the practice and giving her and Jane a pittance compared to the money he had inherited. And he'd been planning on keeping it for himself and that bimbo he played pickleball with?

The unfairness, the stupidity, the utter hatefulness of her father's actions made her so tense that she got up and walked around the room. When she finally made herself get back in bed, she still couldn't sleep. The more she thought, the more helpless she felt. She was going to lose control over her career and the dental practice; she was going to lose all the land and money she'd always assumed belonged to the family. She doubted Robin Carpenter would ever remarry. Why would she, if it meant losing

Bert's multimillion-dollar trust? Instead, Robin could do what so many women did: forget marriage and just live with a guy.

Katherine would, she knew, also lose the money her father was leaving to her mother—Jane was such a spendthrift that even that amount of money would be gone in a year or two.

A sudden sense of panic made her so nauseous that she ran to the bathroom and vomited.

Back in bed, she made up her mind. That woman Robin Carpenter. She had to be stopped. *But how?*

* * *

Katherine had never hesitated to cheat when necessary. She justified it by telling herself she had learned from her dad. She had repeatedly heard him brag about how he could inflate what he charged his patients and shortchange his suppliers. The latter in particular were his favorite targets.

Katherine had pulled similar stunts, but in her own way. She'd cheated at tennis and she'd cheated during tests in biology, chemistry, and physics so often and without getting caught that she'd ended up graduating from high school in the top ten scholastically. But her coup was getting elected prom queen. No one ever knew that she had snuck into the principal's office and changed all those ballots.

No, she was an excellent cheater. And she could do this too. She just had to figure out how.

Chapter Eleven

～

Wednesday morning was everything Lew was expecting and worse. The minute she arrived at work shortly after six, she dispatched three deputies to the Loon Lake Rifle Range to help Bruce and his investigators test the rifles that had been used Tuesday morning. She wouldn't be surprised if one of them had rounds matching the bullet the forensic pathologist had found during the autopsy on Bert Willoughby.

Twenty-two people had used the shooting range that morning, so she knew it would take a while to locate the gun owners and arrange for them to bring their rifles in to be examined. Further complicating the morning were calls from media out of Wausau and Madison requesting information on "the investigation of a possible homicide involving a prominent Northwoods businessman."

It was nine thirty before she was able to sit down with Dani and Judith to review the anonymous tips they'd received during the day Tuesday.

"Four of the five I got are worthless," said Dani, leaning over her notes as she pushed her long curls back behind her ears. "I recognized their voices from the hair salon, and I can tell you these are women who love to gossip. They're just calling in who they *think* would have shot Dr. Willoughby. No proof. But I do have one that you may want to check out, Sheriff Ferris."

Lew smiled to herself. Dani loved to call her Sheriff Ferris when on the job, even though Lew had urged her to use her first name. Lew had said, "We've worked together so long and so closely that we're family, Dani. We're more than boss and employee." But Dani insisted. Lew suspected she liked the idea that she worked for the person in the most senior law enforcement position, which made her own title as head of IT all the more prestigious. If it made her happy, Lew didn't mind. Dani was very good at her job, and that was all the mattered.

"This one person—I'm sure it's a woman, though she sounded pretty scratchy, like on a bad phone or a bad connection," said Dani, excitement building in her voice. "She said her ex-husband is 'a real crook himself'—her exact words—but Doc Willoughby still took him for over ten grand. 'You don't do that to Teddy Curran and get away with it' is what she said. Convinced me," said Dani with raised eyebrows. "You gotta follow up on that one for sure."

"Now, Dani, you know I think Dr. Willoughby's death was most likely an accident," said Lew.

"I know, I know, but that lady is convinced that Teddy Curran has had it in for Dr. Willoughby. She also said he skipped town yesterday, and *that*—to her, anyway—means he's guilty. Now, I did a quick check to see if he has a record, and he does, but it's all related to theft. Specifically, people hire him for roofing and stuff and pay him half up front, only to have the guy disappear and not do the work. But like I said, Sheriff Ferris, he is worth checking out. I have her name and number so we can find her—and hopefully her Teddy, I'm sure."

Lew nodded. Then she turned to the woman who was her administrative right hand. "Judith, you've been too quiet. Got a good candidate too?"

"Very good, Lew, even if indications are that the shooting may have been an accident. I heard from a woman who called me anonymously at my home last night. She knows I work for you. Like Dani, I recognized her voice but didn't say anything. She's a neighbor, in fact, so I don't know what she was thinking not giving me her name. But she is sure the person who shot Bert Willoughby is a woman, a widow, who sued him for malpractice and lost—"

The office door slammed open just as Judith was opening her mouth to say more. A man in a Loon Lake Police Department uniform barged in waving a torn sheet of paper.

"Jeez, Officer Adamczyk, *slow down*," said Lew, getting to her feet. "What on earth?"

"Sheriff! You gotta see this. Right now—"

"Calm down, Roger, before you have a heart attack," said Lew as she came around her desk.

"This note was under my wipers. Someone stuck it there while I was checking parking meters half an hour ago. Here, see for yourself what it says." He thrust the torn piece of paper at Lew.

She looked down to read what had been handwritten with a black marker: *Robin Steadman shot Bert Willoughby. She did it for the money.*

Lew glanced over at Dani and Judith. "Whoever wrote this must think I drive Officer Adamczyk's squad car and spend the county's money checking parking meters. That's absurd—"

"Or that whatever police officer was using that vehicle could certainly get the message to you," said Judith. Her natural kindness was something Lew liked about her.

"Well," said Lew, feeling chastened as she gave Roger Adamczyk a reassuring pat on the shoulder and walked back to her chair, "the message has definitely gotten to me. Thank you, Officer Adamczyk. Now, please calm down. Okay?"

With a nod and a look on his face that signified he knew he had accomplished a critical mission, the older man nodded and hurried out of the office.

Lew turned back to Judith. "You were saying?"

"My neighbor said this widow she knows hates Bert Willoughby with a passion. Her late husband was seeing him for painful sores on his tongue. Dr. Willoughby, who was their family dentist, dismissed his symptoms as typical of old age and said he'd get over it. And gave him some prescription.

"Well, it did get worse, and when they were on vacation in Florida and he couldn't swallow, the dentist he saw there diagnosed it immediately: cancer of the tongue. But it was too late, already stage four, and it had spread to his lymph nodes in his neck. He had surgery, but it left him unable to speak. After he died, his widow sued Willoughby for malpractice and lost."

Judith shook her head. "She doesn't hate Bert because of losing the lawsuit but for losing her husband," she said. "And one more thing my neighbor thinks you should know: the husband and wife enjoyed bird hunting together. They often shot trap to keep their shooting skills sharp. She said she could see the widow taking him down with one bullet easy."

As Judith was talking, Lew reflected again on how fortunate she was to have the older woman as her "chief admin," which was what everyone called her. Judith Hanson had grown up in Loon Lake but spent her career in the printing industry north of Milwaukee. On retiring from her position in senior management, she'd returned to her parents' home in Loon Lake, which she had inherited and held on to over the years.

There was a reason for her return, and it had nothing to do with nostalgia: Judith had been determined to find the answer to the murder of her older sister thirty years before. To the surprise of her family, rather than relaxing into her retirement, she'd applied to assist Dani, the IT tech for the Loon Lake Police Department. While Judith told Lew and Dani that she was "interested in staying current with the technological advances in the print and data arenas," her real reason for taking the job was her hope that working with law enforcement might offer her a window to the facts, if not the truth, surrounding her sister's death.

Not only did Judith's work with Dani lead to uncovering the details that her parents had hidden from her, but she discovered a new sense of enthusiasm in working with Lewellyn Ferris and her other Loon Lake Police colleagues. When her sister's murder was solved shortly before Lew Ferris was elected sheriff of McBride County, Judith faced a decision: retire again, or take on a new position as chief admin for Sheriff Lewellyn Ferris. She didn't hesitate—she took the job.

"This is very interesting information," said Lew, thinking over everything Judith had just told her. Her cell phone rang, and she looked down to see who was calling, "It's Bruce," she said, taking the call.

"No luck yet," said Bruce Peters. "I'm here with my guys at the sports club, and we have a good dozen more to examine, but I thought you'd like an update. Also, I stopped up at those old tennis courts before I came over here. Ray was still searching through the brush and the old pines. He said he'd had no luck. I'll let you know when we finish up here."

The instant Lew ended the call with Bruce, the woman working dispatch rushed into her office, a frantic expression on her face. "Sheriff Ferris, can you please take a call? I have a woman hysterical on the phone demanding to speak to you. She says she has the gun that shot Dr. Willoughby—"

"She what?" Lew interrupted the woman.

"She said she has the gun. She has called in three times. I tried to tell her I'd have someone call her shortly, that you were in a meeting—"

"It's okay, Arlene, put her through," said Lew, looking over at Judith and Dani with her eyebrows raised. "A nut, I'm sure," she said in a whisper.

As soon as she heard the call click through, Lew said, "Hello?" in her professional voice.

"Yes, it's me. We talked yesterday morning." The voice was harsh, rising in volume.

Lew held the phone away with a puzzled look on her face. Whoever it was sounded familiar. . . .

"It's Jane Willoughby, for God's sake," the caller shouted, apparently sensing Lew's confusion.

"Oh, yes, Jane. What's this about a gun?"

"I have the gun. That woman. She brought the gun here—after she shot my husband."

Arlene was right: Jane Willoughby was hysterical.

Chapter Twelve

❧

"All right, Mrs. Willoughby," Lew said, her voice calm and soothing. "I hear you, and I'll be right over. It will take a few minutes. If what you say is true, I need to bring one of the experts from the Wausau Crime Lab with me. Once I pick him up, we'll be right over. I'm going to hang up now and call the expert. Will you be okay? This could take twenty minutes."

"Yes. Hurry. That woman will run—"

"I'll be there shortly, and we'll make sure no one goes anywhere."

"Can we do anything?" asked Judith as Lew punched in Bruce's cell number.

Lew shook her head. "Thank you; just keep track of the rest of these calls. The woman may be crazy, but she's the victim's widow, so I'll listen."

When Lew drove up to the firing range minutes later, Bruce was ready. As he climbed into the passenger seat, he said, "I have one of my guys ready to follow us. He's great on ballistics and may be able to eyeball the situation and let us know if we should be testing the gun ASAP."

As he spoke, his bushy eyebrows knit together across his brow, making him look like someone you would never want to cross. Lew found that humorous, as she knew Bruce was so softhearted that he was emotionally stressed when he hooked a brook trout—worried that his barbless trout fly might damage the poor fish's mouth. She had never seen anyone take such care releasing his tiny trophy. Another reason she liked the guy.

"Good," said Lew, checking her rearview mirror to be sure the ballistics guy was behind them. "I have a very upset individual to deal with, so let's hope we can calm things down."

Jane Willoughby was waiting in her doorway and waved them in, her arms again moving in frantic circles. She led them into the foyer, past the gleaming, curved oak stairwell and into the darkened side room holding Bert Willoughby's gun collection. Marching straight to the wall of gun racks, the woman made no move to turn on a light. Frustrated, Lew searched for a light switch and flicked it on before saying, "Mrs. Willoughby, please take a moment for me to introduce everyone. This is Bruce Peters, chief investigator for the Wausau Crime Lab, and Ron Schauder, his ballistics expert. Now, please show us the gun you think was used to shoot your husband."

"I don't *think*—I *know* it was this one."

Grabbing the gun closest to her by its stock, Jane shoved it at Ron Schauder. Schauder's eyes widened, and he backed a few steps away before reaching to take the gun from the woman. After studying the Browning rifle, Ron asked, "Mrs. Willoughby, do you have cartridges for this gun?"

"Maybe? What the hell's a cartridge? Let me look in that drawer there. I never touch anything in this room . . ." As she was yanking the drawer open, a tall woman, younger but large and big boned, walked in the front door. Her face was tight with concern. "What's happening? Mom? Are you all right?"

"Don't ask stupid questions," said Jane, barking in a loud voice as she kept her back to her daughter.

"What are you doing?" asked Katherine, staring at the three people standing there.

"Your mother insists one of these guns was used to shoot your father," said Lew. "She called my office, and I've assured her we will check it out—"

"You need to check out that goddamn Robin Steadman," said Jane, interrupting Lew.

"Mom, please, you got this all wrong," said Katherine, walking into the gun room with her hands up as if to quiet her mother. "I tried to tell you in the lawyer's office, but you wouldn't listen—"

"No, dammit, *you* got it wrong."

In a voice short of a scream but louder than her mother's, Katherine managed to be heard: *"Mom. Shut. Up."*

The room went silent.

"The woman who gets Dad's money is Robin *Carpenter*, not Robin Steadman. You got the two women mixed up."

Jane stared at her daughter for a long, long moment. Then she turned and stomped out of the room. Within seconds, somewhere in the house, a door slammed.

Katherine turned to the group. She pointed at the rifle that Ron Schauder was holding. "No one used that gun to shoot anyone," she said. "My dad and his dental assistant, Robin Steadman, often used it to shoot critters when they needed to. Dad would use it at his deer shack to shoot beavers, and Robin had borrowed it because she had a weasel getting into her chicken coop." As she was speaking, Ron Schauder walked over to set the gun back on the rack.

"What happened yesterday morning was that my mother—after she got the news of Dad's death—demanded I take her to see our family lawyer. She bullied that poor man into telling her what's in my dad's will—"

Seeing both Lew and Bruce open their mouths to speak, she put up a hand to stop them. "I know, I know. But Mom bullied the poor man into telling her what we all know we'll hear in probate anyhow. Yes, he may have broken a law, but that had to be less painful than listening to my mom." Katherine grimaced. "He told her that my dad was planning to file for divorce—"

"Really?" asked Lew, surprised.

"Nothing new, trust me," said Katherine. "My parents' marriage thrived on constant fighting and threats to divorce each other. That was daily life around here, and that's why I don't live here. I have my own place.

"But what *did* surprise both Mom and me was the news that he recently wrote a new will, one different from anything he had with my mom. That really upset my mom. Dad's new will leaves some money to this woman who was his pickleball partner. Her name is Robin too, so that's when Mom jumped to the conclusion it was Robin *Stead-man* and not the other one. She wouldn't let me correct her."

Katherine gave them a sheepish look. "I know. It sounds stupid, but you try to get a word in edgewise when my mother is ranting . . ."

"We weren't there," said Lew. "Believe me, I know how things get twisted when people are upset. You don't have to apologize."

"Thank you," said Katherine. "I am really so sorry about all this."

"Not to worry," said Bruce as Ron nodded in agreement.

"I do think your father was shot by accident," said Lew, "but these gentlemen and their colleagues are the experts, and they'll be able to confirm if I'm right or not."

"Thank you all for putting up with this," said Katherine as she walked them to the front door. "My mother can be difficult. She has her own ideas, and good luck changing her mind."

As Katherine was turning away, Lew was surprised to see a smug expression flash across the woman's face. Was she happy that others were now aware of her mother's eccentric behavior?

Lew wanted to ask more questions. Had Jane been aware that her husband was sincere in filing for divorce this time? Had she thought he was having an affair? *Mind your own business*, Lew told herself. All that had nothing to do with Bert Willoughby's death.

Still, as she drove, she couldn't help thinking about that smug look on Katherine Willoughby's face. She wanted to ask her, *Are you happy to have people see your mother as a nutcase?* Then she chastised herself again, remembering a comment she had once heard: *Every family has its own special kind of dysfunction.*

After Lew dropped Bruce and Ron Schauder off at the firing range, she decided to drive back along Loon Lake Road to where it led to the old boys' camp. As she rounded the curves and glanced down the side roads leading to lake properties that had been built along the five-lake chain—cottages, summer homes, and now year-round homes—she was reminded of how property values in the Northwoods were changing.

In the early 1900s when wealthy families from Milwaukee and Chicago and Detroit took the train or drove north for summer vacations, they tended to build their summer places on the lakes further north or west—lakes much deeper and with sparkling clear water. The demand for property was so great that cottages and expensive summer homes were crowded onto small lots and often constructed quite close together.

The Loon Lake chain of lakes held dark water caused by the tannins from the tamarack trees that grew in the wetlands bordering the lakes. This made the Loon Lake properties less desirable. It also made land cheaper. Here the summer homes and cottages often had more than an acre between them, which allowed for more privacy.

Until recently, that is. The arrival of invasive plant species that thrived in clear water had led to clogged waterways. Suddenly, the highly prized summer hot spots were no longer so hot.

Now the lakes with tamarack trees and dark water, not hospitable to plants like Eurasian water milfoil, had become more desirable. The Loon Lake chain in particular had become popular for water-skiing, paddleboarding, and fishing. Tourists eager to avoid waterways that clogged the propellers of their speedboats were eager to invest in the properties along the road where Lew was driving.

The Loon Lake homeowners still had large lots, although that appeared to be changing. One section looked like a small town, with modest family homes on both sides of a street that ran down to the water.

At one intersection, Lew pulled over, thinking. Off to her right, a black-topped town road led down past the parking lot for a rustic bar and disappeared. She knew from taking walks with Osborne that the road led to a summer home a good quarter-mile away. It would be wise to check on roads like that, she thought, and made a mental note to ask Ray to follow up. A person living at a distance from other homes might be tempted to sight a rifle on a target on their own property, thinking it would be safe. However, Lew's faith in the wisdom of humanity had been tested often enough that she knew someone who would do something so stupid might not realize that missing their target could send their bullet in a direction dangerous to someone hundreds of yards away.

She reached for her cell phone to call Ray, only to have a familiar face appear in the window of her cruiser.

"Doc? What are you doing here?"

"No, what are *you* doing here? Forget my address?" Before she could answer, he said, "I'm on my way back from dropping off a cane pole at the home of an old friend whose grandson snarled his fishing line so bad only an expert could fix it." Osborne grinned. "But, hey, what are you up to? Anything I can help with?"

Lew told him her thoughts on someone sighting a gun in their own backyard. "Doc, what do you think?"

"Yep," said Osborne with a nod. "Sure could happen. I know one of my buddies was grouse hunting and grazed a bow hunter sitting in a tree stand almost a mile away. Bow season for deer had opened early that year. Didn't hurt the bow hunter but scared the bejesus out of my friend. And he had no way of seeing that guy because he was so far away." He nodded again. "Yes, good idea to check that out, Lewellyn. Ray can do it, or I will. But, more important right now— come for dinner, won't you? I know it's the night we stay at our own places, but you've been going all day. I stopped by to have my morning coffee with you, and they said you'd already left. Take a break and have dinner at my place, kiddo."

Lew gave him a grateful smile. "I will do just that. You're right. What time is it? I even forgot to have lunch."

* * *

By five o'clock Lew was ready to call it a day. The stack of reports was still high, the list of calls to be returned was untouched, but she was exhausted. She knew she could whip through it all if she got a good night's sleep.

As she walked toward her cruiser in the parking lot, her cell phone rang. She looked at the name of the caller: Barbara Steadman, her best friend since childhood.

"Barbara, what a surprise—"

"Lewellyn, my daughter Robin is getting death threats."

Chapter Thirteen

An hour later Lew found herself sitting at Osborne's kitchen table and listening to Robin Steadman's voice break as she described a series of threatening phone calls and a scribbled note stuck under the windshield of her SUV. Her mother sat beside her, holding her hand and gently rubbing her back as she spoke.

"Do you recognize the voice?" Lew asked.

"Of course I do," said Robin with a catch in her throat. "It's Mrs. Willoughby, my boss's wife. She's convinced I shot her husband. I mean, it's ridiculous. I've tried to calm her down, but—" Robin heaved a sigh and paused.

"Have the calls stopped?"

"Yeah, a couple hours ago. I'm worried she'll start up again—or come to my house . . ."

Stroking her daughter's back, Barbara said, "I told Robin not to worry. I'll stay with her until you can do something about this, Lew. You can, right?"

"Yes, and I'll have one of my deputies keep an eye on Robin's place tonight and for the next couple of days. But I also know Jane Willoughby was given information this afternoon—by her daughter, Katherine—that you, Robin, are not the woman she suspected of having an affair with her husband. That individual is also named Robin, which is what this is all about. So Jane Willoughby was confused—"

"*Confused?* Out of her mind is more like it," said Barbara, incensed. "How do we know she's not going to call again or stalk my daughter? Lewellyn, she should be arrested."

Robin turned to her mother. "Now *you* calm down," she said with a halfhearted chuckle. "You're starting to sound like Mrs. Willoughby, Mom."

Lew was relieved to hear that Robin understood how she had been mistakenly targeted. "Mrs. Willoughby is pretty emotional on a good day," Robin said, smiling through the tears she was wiping off her cheeks. "Thinking I was the pickleball player and not the Robin running the dental office—that doesn't surprise me, really."

"Nor me," said Osborne, chiming in from where he was standing at the stove, warming a pot of chili, while listening to the women. "She was a close friend of my late wife. They were in the same bridge and garden clubs . . ." He paused to stir the chili. The women at the table waited in silence for him to continue. "Two more mean-spirited females it would be hard to find."

"Your wife was like that?" Robin's eyes widened.

"She was. I hate to say it, but it's true." Osborne dropped his head, thinking, then added, "I won't go on about this, but my daughters and I have realized that we put up with some . . . aberrant behavior." He glanced over at Barbara. "I know you and Lewellyn are close friends, so I'm sure she's told you I'm a recovering alcoholic and I've been through the Hazelden Betty Ford Foundation clinic. Saved my life and opened my eyes to what my daughters and I had been living with—the criticism, the isolation, the lack of basic kindness. Not to mention humor." Osborne smiled to lighten the impact of what he had just said.

"Yes, Lew's told me. I hope that's all right."

"Oh, of course," said Osborne with a laugh. "But back to Jane Willoughby for a minute. Women like Jane—and like Mary Lee—have a bad habit of making up their minds before they hear the whole story. I'm sure Jane heard your first name and that was that."

"But her daughter, Katherine, jumped right in when she tried to repeat that misinformation this afternoon," Lew said. "And Katherine did not hold back. She made it clear to her mother that you had nothing to do with the accident, Robin."

Seeing relief on Robin's face, Lew decided to push for more information. "I have a question for you, now that you know you have a protector in Jane's daughter. What is she like? I know you run the day-to-day in the dental office, so you must interact with her a fair amount. Is she a good person to work with?"

Robin tipped her head sideways, giving some thought before she spoke. Watching her, Lew couldn't get over how much she resembled her mother: both wore their curly light-brown hair short and tucked behind their ears. *And they have the same ears*, thought Lew with a silent chuckle. Barbara had put on at least thirty pounds since they were teenagers together, but mother and daughter were the same height, Robin being the slimmer version.

Lew had known Barbara since they were neighbors and walked to middle school together, becoming best friends. Fate worked in strange ways, and their friendship had been a gift triggered by a devastating family tragedy: Lew's parents were killed one night in a car accident on icy roads. She and her older brother moved in with their grandfather, a widower who owned a sporting goods store in their hometown. And that was when Lew met Barbara, who lived next door.

Years later, Lew was there to help when Barbara's husband, Rick, was battling terminal cancer. She took young Robin into her home with her own two children for the final difficult weeks. Not long after that, when Lew was going through a difficult divorce from her alcoholic husband, Barbara was there to listen and to provide a place where Lew and her children could escape the troubling behavior in their home.

Before Lew took the job with the Loon Lake Police and right after Barbara had gotten her degree in library science, the two often spent their weekends at each other's homes. Even now, years later, they chatted by phone at least once a month.

Next to Osborne, Barbara was Lew's closest friend. It hadn't taken long for Barbara to see that Paul Osborne had found in Lew a dear friend as well as a sweetheart. A keen observer, she had a hunch that the relationship was a first for the man who had grown up with no model for what a good marriage could be—or should be. Over the last three years, she had developed a deep bond of friendship with the man too. If Lew loved him, she loved him.

Hearing Lew's questions about Katherine Willoughby, Barbara encouraged her daughter, saying, "Go ahead, hon. Tell Lew and Doc what you've told me. And don't hold back—this is no time to be polite."

"Okay, Mom, I hear you," said Robin. After a brief pause, she said, "What I'm about to say is more about feelings than facts, and all this is based on my observations, so I could be wrong."

"We hear you," said Lew, nodding to encourage her.

"Well, for one thing, I know Katherine and her mother don't get along—"

"Who could?" asked Osborne, interrupting. "Sorry, didn't mean to be rude, Robin."

Robin gave him a reassuring look. "It's okay. Our entire office knows Jane—and how to handle her. The good news is she rarely shows up there. No, it's Bert's attitude that I worried about. For one thing, he was quite irritated when Katherine first told him she wanted to join the practice. He made it clear to me that he did not want that. In fact, he asked me to try to persuade her to join a practice down in Wausau. But she persisted, and she *is* family, so . . ."

"Was he okay after she started seeing patients?" asked Osborne.

"Kind of. He certainly made room for her and asked me to assist when she needed someone. But he went cheap on the equipment and was dismissive."

"Dismissive?" said Lew. "How do you mean, exactly?"

"He had no interest in what she was doing. Even when she asked for his advice, he'd shove her off on me or another dentist for help. It was like she wasn't there. Frankly, I think he's always treated her that way. Again, this is strictly my opinion, and I'm no family therapist but . . . and I'm sorry to say this . . . but I really think that Bert did not like his daughter.

"But—and please remember, this is just my opinion— she's kind of a know-it-all and bossy like her mother. In a way, I couldn't blame him. Happy family, right?" Robin managed a tight-lipped grin.

"He liked you better?" Lew asked the question and then wished she hadn't.

Robin looked at her. "Yes. I know he saw me as a friend. Sad thing is, he was never friendly towards Katherine, at least not in the same way. And she knows that. I see it in her eyes when she asks me for help. More than once she has asked for something and said 'I know Dad doesn't think this is important, but . . .'"

"I wonder why she chose to come back to Loon Lake?" Lew said.

Lips pursed, Robin tipped her head up, thinking for a moment. "You know, I don't think Katherine fits in *any-where*. I don't hear her talking about friends or doing things with other people. I have to wonder if she was lonely as a kid and this is all she knows. She may not be happy practicing with her father, but she knows the territory. She's comfortable."

"And she doesn't live with happy Jane . . ." Osborne couldn't resist.

"Right. She doesn't have to live with her mother," said Robin, agreeing.

"All right, ladies, dinner awaits," said Osborne. He had made chili and a salad and was eager to move the evening along. He could see the exhaustion on Lew's face.

* * *

Listening to the three women talk, Osborne had reflected on the remarkable differences between Lew and Barbara— and yet they were best friends. Barbara was petite, almost tiny. Though she had put on weight over the years, she was still a small woman. Her light-brown hair, streaked gray, made her look even more girlish.

Lew, on the other hand, was a good four inches taller than her friend, wide in the shoulders and hips, full chested, sturdy, and strong. The short, dark curls she brushed back from her face emphasized her dark eyes and prominent features. She and Barbara were a study in opposites.

Once, when Lew described herself to Osborne as stocky, he had countered with "No, you are lithe and shapely, my dear—very sexy." And she had punched him in the arm, her eyes sparkling.

What made her friendship with Barbara unique, Lew had explained, was that they were "on the same wavelength" when it came to knowing people. Over the years, the two women had been there for one another through deaths, divorces, and the satisfaction of finding themselves in careers that made them feel not only happy but appreciated.

What they shared was deep friendship, a friendship worth more than money. And one similar to what he hoped to share with Lew for a long, long time.

As he and Lew lay in bed that night, she said, "I hope I was some help to Barbara and Robin. Getting angry phone calls like that is upsetting. And Robin is like her mom—so kind. It's so not fair, Doc. If I were nine years old again, I'd punch Jane out."

Osborne couldn't help chuckling as he wrapped his arms around her and pulled her close. "I'm sure you would. Problem is, she'd punch back, and then where would you be?"

"You're right. But I do have to do *something* about it."

"My opinion," said Osborne, "is to let it drop. Now that Jane knows she made a mistake, she'll back off."

"I hope you're right." Lew lay quiet, thinking. "You know, Barbara and I have been there for each other at critical times. When her husband was dying of cancer; when mine was being so ugly during the divorce. I want to make this right for her and for Robin. I can't do much right now, so I hope she knows that."

"She does. She sees it in your eyes. Your friend knows you're there for both of them."

Just as I hope you'll be there for me, thought Osborne, looking through the bedroom window at the pines swaying in the night breeze.

He was almost asleep when Lew piped up, "Tomorrow will fix it." She said it as if trying to convince herself. "Bruce's guys will confirm that someone sighted their gun in the wrong direction. That should put an end to this Willoughby baloney."

"Try to get some sleep," said Osborne, patting her shoulder.

"Hmm," was all he heard.

* * *

Early Thursday morning, Deb Wallace pulled into her parking spot behind the Willoughbys' garage. She liked to get started on housework around six thirty, before Jane started messing around.

Slipping through the back door, she hung her fleece jacket on one of the back porch hooks before reaching for the long-handled feather duster. It was the duster Jane liked to use on the antique Chinese vases she kept on top of the armoire on the second-floor landing. "No, no, Deb, only I can dust those," she would say whenever Deb offered to help. "They are very, very valuable." As if Deb planned to smash the dang things.

"Right, just like Bert's goddamn guns," Deb would mutter to herself. He'd never let her touch those either. But today was different. Bert was gone, and the gun collection was gathering dust. Deb knew it was her job to keep things tidy, so unless Bert rose from the dead, the guns were getting dusted. She didn't need to wait until Jane complained and then shorted her twenty bucks for "forgetting."

Walking into the room that housed the gun collection, she noticed one was missing. It was the Browning that Bert and Robin Steadman used on critters. *Oh,* she thought, *Robin must have borrowed it again.* As she worked, she saw that the drawer below the rack where the Browning usually sat was half-open. She shoved it closed.

Chapter Fourteen

Diane Knutsen, a graduate student in environmental sciences who was interning at the university's Outdoors Science Center, inched her Camry along the back loop of Loon Lake Road, her eyes scanning the grasses and brush lining the road for the path to her ruffed grouse trap.

The section of road where she was driving had morphed into a dirt lane that served only one old cottage, which someone had been built out on the peninsula separating Loon Lake from the next lake in the chain of five lakes. The old cottage had been there since sometime back in the early 1900s, and Diane would have sworn the dirt lane was that old too. Since the property was privately owned, the town had never paved or maintained the road. Why it was even called a road was beyond her. What remained was barely discernible and used mainly by people lost and needing a place to turn around—perfect hiding places for ruffed grouse.

She had found the path leading off the dirt lane twice before, so she was sure she could find it again. She knew it was one of two paths that ran around the old boys' camp, but the grounds were so overgrown that the paths were seldom used, and then mainly by cable TV repairmen searching for squirrel damage to their aboveground lines.

At least they thought it was squirrels. As Diane had learned more about the grouse and other animals hiding in the young aspen that were overtaking the property, she'd begun to wonder if it wasn't fishers—members of the weasel family that had been known to prey on family cats. "Vicious little guys," she muttered, thinking out loud as she drove.

Eyes searching along the grassy bank, she winced in frustration as she became aware of the sun rising over the lake to her left. She had intended to be doing this an hour earlier but had made the mistake of closing her eyes one more minute this morning. A minute that turned into thirty . . .

Whoa—there it was. She drove another fifty yards to a clearing off to her right where she could leave the car. Grabbing her grouse kit, she walked back down the lane to the barely discernible path. The morning breeze felt so good on her face that she wished every morning could be like this. Then she reminded herself that it was September and that the morning breeze would soon be icy.

She had until spring to complete her native study on how winter conditions influenced the ruffed grouse populations in the Northwoods: where they lived, how long they lived, whether their numbers increased, and, if not, what might help. She loved her work.

Aha! The bright-yellow stake she had planted two trips ago showed up on her right. She walked slowly and cautiously off the path toward her first trap of the morning. Dropping to her knees, she crawled through the branches and undergrowth of the young trees as quietly as possible, hoping, hoping. . . .

Her heart dropped: the trap was empty. Crawling closer to the long, low chicken-wire fence that she had built that summer, she kept hoping. Ah, fifteen feet later, and right where the trap funneled into what she liked to call her "capture pen," she saw a flash of feathers. *Success.* She heaved a heavy sigh as she reached for her kit.

At that moment, she heard a noise behind her—feet moving along the path in her direction. Someone from the science center? Maybe. Maybe one of her colleagues had forgotten she was planning to check the five traps today. Knowing the grouse in the pen couldn't escape until she released it, she paused to listen. The footsteps went on by without stopping.

Hmm, she thought. Must be a runner who liked the old path because it kept them off the paved road, with its tight curves and sloppy drivers. Remembering that the path snaked up and around the camp's old tennis courts, she expected the runner to circle up and head back in her direction. She made a mental note not to pop up and scare them.

Turning back to the grouse, she reached in for the bird. She wanted to complete the banding as fast as possible to avoid traumatizing her tiny prize. Working quickly, she weighed and measured the feathered body, then attached the leg band. Next was the collar, which carried an accelerometer that tracked the bird's movements, and a radio, which would emit a VHF signal so she could track its location. Once that was done, she would be able to regularly check on the bird's movements and update her log. If done correctly, the accelerometer would then store the data showing the bird's activity, which she could analyze for her study. *Whew. Done.*

One last chore—if she had to call it that: collect a tail feather and take photos of the bird's tail fan and wings. The feather in hand, she pulled her iPhone from her back pocket and held the bird and the phone high to catch enough sunlight that the tail fan would be illuminated, making it easy to study.

She had just taken the photo of the tail fan when she heard what was unmistakably a gunshot. Then another. Close by. Her breath caught and she stayed perfectly still, hands high.

She could hear the runner coming her way and turned, phone in hand, to watch the person, hoping they hadn't been hurt. From where she was, twenty feet or more from the path, she could see the figure running. The person was wearing a top with a hood that appeared to cover their face. In their left hand they were carrying something long. A branch to defend themselves? As the runner neared, Diane saw the rifle.

Her phone still held high, her index finger pressed hard on the camera button. It pinged multiple times before she realized what she was doing. The person with the gun stopped. *Had they heard her camera?* She wished she'd had the sound turned off.

Falling to her knees and slipping the bird back into the funnel, she rolled under the branches of the young aspen and stopped breathing. Silence.

Then footsteps in her direction . . .

Was she about to die?

The footsteps stopped. Had the person seen the yellow stake and turned toward it? The path was so indistinct, they may have thought they'd made a wrong turn. She heard a scrambling in the brush and waited for the figure to show up and stand over her.

Again she heard footsteps, running now—running away.

Diane let herself breathe.

She got to her knees, still waiting. No sound.

What to do?

Maybe this was nothing? Maybe the runner was someone looking to shoot squirrels? Or raccoons? Other critters people considered pests? Maybe one of those doggone fishers? Maybe target practice? She knew deer season wasn't far off. In fact, she would have to stop checking her traps during that time so she wouldn't get shot.

She looked down at the grouse, who looked back at her as if to say *I'm ready—is it time to let me go?* With a smile of relief, she reached for the bird and, turning toward the path, released it. Good, a great start to the day.

After putting her phone away and the banding equipment back into her kit, she got to her feet and started to push her way through aspen. At the path, she paused. She decided to take ten minutes and see where that runner had been when they were firing their rifle, if only to warn her colleagues that the area was being used for target practice.

As she got closer to the old camp, she saw the lodge, which had been built of long Norway pine logs. The dark roof had a blue tarp covering a section that must have collapsed in. So sad to see a historic old place like that fall into disrepair, she thought. She loved the old log buildings.

The tall wire fencing surrounding the old tennis courts was sagging, with large holes in sections. The courts themselves had large cracks where they were disintegrating. As she peered through the branches of the tall balsams surrounding the courts, she could make out a dark bundle on the court farthest from where she was standing. A bear cub, maybe? Was that what had stopped the runner? Gosh, she couldn't believe someone would shoot a young bear. The cub would be more afraid of the human.

She stepped onto the tennis court farthest from the bundle. If the animal was alive, she needed to be careful. She inched forward. No movement. She got closer. She stopped for a moment, then ran, reaching for her phone.

The woman on the court had fallen forward into netting that had gone down with the weight of her body. Her head was black with blood, and blood was pooling around her upper body.

Diane hit 911 on her phone. "Someone—a tennis player," she cried, "has been shot. They aren't moving. Please send help! Here, on the tennis court by that old boys' camp. You know—at the end of Loon Lake Road."

Shaking, she walked closer and knelt beside the still figure. "It's okay," she said softly. "Lie still. Don't move. They're coming to help. You'll be okay."

No response. A siren could already be heard. Diane kept breathing, refusing to look around, refusing to think the runner with the rifle might have returned.

It was six thirty Thursday morning.

Chapter Fifteen

⁓

Lew pulled into her parking space at the sheriff's department just in time to hear the scream of an ambulance siren as it pulled out of the EMT parking area, which was located a block away behind St. Mary's Hospital. Walking into the McBride County Building where her offices were located, she stopped at the dispatch counter, just inside the entrance.

With a nod back toward the parking lot, she asked Marlaine on dispatch, "What's that about? Car accident?'

"Just sending you the alert, Sheriff Ferris—got it from the 911 center a second ago. Possible shooting out on Loon Lake Road. From what my friend working 911 said, the caller didn't know exactly where they were, but it might be that old boys' camp—"

Before Marlaine could say another word, Lew was out the door.

*   *   *

As she sped toward Loon Lake Road, Lew called Bruce Peters, hoping he'd pick up, although she knew he must have gotten home to Wausau late last night. A sleepy voice answered. "Hey, Sheriff, out fishing a blue olive hatch this early?"

"Are you sleeping?"

"And talking in my sleep? Sure."

"No, serious, Bruce. I'm following an ambulance out to the boys' camp, where someone else has been shot. No details yet, but please answer when I call back. Okay?"

"Only if there's a decent mayfly hatch. Sorry, bad joke. Yes, standing by. I mean, sleeping by."

"Thank you," said Lew as she clicked off. She had a hunch this was not going to be good. And though she knew that, as the county sheriff, she had a half dozen deputies she could have called on to follow the ambulance, she felt better handling this herself. And pushing papers on her desk got old.

The sense of foreboding grew as her cruiser rounded a corner just a mile from the camp. She knew in her gut that with two people shot near the old boys' camp, something was not right.

*   *   *

After parking her cruiser on the dirt road beside the ambulance, she hurried in the direction of the old tennis courts, where she could see a small crowd had gathered: two EMTs in uniform and one other person. She hadn't gone far when she became aware of two cars pulling over to park on the road near her cruiser. Three people dressed in shorts, T-shirts, and light fleece jackets got out and headed her way.

"Stop, please. Wait right where you are. We have an emergency." She put her arms out to stop them.

"We're here to practice pickleball," said a tall man, craning his neck to look past her. "What's happened over there? Somebody get hurt? Hope it's not Robin. She's our best player—"

"You have to stop and wait right here," said Lew, her voice louder as she repeated herself while flashing her badge.

"Oh, sorry," said the man, backing off. "I'm supposed to meet my partner here. I hope she's okay . . ." But Lew was running off toward the courts before he could finish.

As she approached the small cluster of people on the tennis court, one of the EMTs spotted her coming and waved the others back. "Sheriff Ferris," he said, "thank you for getting here so fast. We have a situation here." He went on to say that they had determined immediately on arriving that the person lying on a patch of broken concrete was no longer breathing. "No pulse," he added. "Shall I call the coroner?"

"Wait," said Lew, holding up a hand. In spite of the blood pooling around the victim's head, she had recognized Robin Carpenter. "What's that wrapped around her?" asked Lew as she motioned for everyone to stand back.

"Pickleball net, I believe," said one of the EMTs. "She fell into it when she was shot, or maybe she was putting it up when it happened."

Lew reached for her cell phone to call the man who had cooked her waffles an hour earlier. He answered immediately, though she could hear a buzz of people in the background. "Doc, can you hear me okay?"

"Yes, what's up, Lew?"

"I need to deputize you as acting coroner and get you out here to the old boys' camp ASAP."

"Pecore in his cups again?" asked Osborne.

"No. The victim is his niece. She's been shot. At least I think she's been shot. I'm going to get Bruce and the Wausau Crime Lab guys up here right away."

"Sure, of course. I'll be right there. I have to stop and grab my kit at the house, though. You caught me down on the dock, working on my boat."

"Fine. But don't say anything to anyone, please?"

"You know I wouldn't." She did know to be cautious about who she spoke to, of course. Maybe she was reminding herself to be careful and not jump to conclusions before she got all the details.

As she turned back to the EMTs, she became aware of the young, dark-haired woman standing with her back against one of the rusted poles holding up the torn wire fencing. She had been watching Lew and the EMTs in silence, her dark eyes worried. Lew walked over to her and said, "I'm the McBride County sheriff, Lew Ferris. Who are you, and why are you here?"

"Diane Knutsen. I found her. I heard gunshots, and then I found her. I'm, ah, I'm a grad student working at the university's Outdoor Science Center, and I was checking my grouse traps when this happened. I called 911."

"So you were standing here when she got shot?"

"Oh, no, I was way back there," said the young woman, pointing into the thicket of aspen and young balsam crowding the tennis court fence. "I had just finished band-ing a ruffed grouse when I heard the gunshot. Then a per-son with a gun ran down the path alongside where I was working, but I thought maybe they were shooting raccoons or something. I had no idea—"

"You were *banding a grouse?*" asked Lew, trying to understand.

"Yes, I'm a grad student studying how winters here in the Northwoods will affect the ruffed grouse population. I have five traps in the area, and I was working with one when—"

"Wait right here," said Lew, interrupting her. "I have to secure this area and make a couple phone calls. Once I have that taken care of, I need you to show me exactly where you were when you heard the gunshots."

Worry dark in her eyes, the girl nodded.

As Lew walked back toward the EMTs, she hit Bruce's number. He answered immediately. "I'm up," he said, speaking briskly. "Need us up there?"

"I do. You know the victim. It's the woman who was playing pickleball with Bert Willoughby when he was shot. The blonde, remember?"

"Of course. After you called, I checked with my office. No one is using our helicopter today, at least not yet, so I'll grab it and one of my guys. I'll have the others drive up. They should be there by eleven. I'll be there within the hour. Do I assume the victim is deceased?"

"Yes."

"So I'll see to transport for forensics and the autopsy too."

"Thanks, Bruce. You get two trips to the Prairie for this, you know." Once off the phone, Lew walked over to the EMTs, who were waiting for directions.

"Bruce Peters from the Wausau Crime Lab should be here within the hour. The other Wausau boys will be here less than two hours from now. Also, Bruce is arranging for the victim to be transported to the Wausau Crime Lab for an autopsy. And I'll call in for deputies to help me secure the area, so you shouldn't have to wait here much longer."

Before walking back to Diane Knutsen, Lew called her office. Judith answered, saying, "Another accident?"

"This is no accident," said Lew, "and the Wausau boys are on their way. But I need you to reach two of my deputies and ask them to get out here as fast as possible. Need them to help me secure the site and keep people away until the Wausau boys have finished their work."

"Done," said Judith.

Once Lew was off the phone, it was less than five minutes before she heard a distant siren—one of the deputies was on the way. She was relieved to see that the three pickleball players had followed her instructions and were waiting by their cars. They weren't leaving, but they weren't causing any problems either.

When the first deputy arrived, Lew made sure he knew how to secure the crime scene before she went to follow up with Diane, the witness.

Once she was able to walk back to the young woman, Lew told her, "Okay, I've arranged for the Wausau boys to be here shortly, so please, show me where you were and what you saw."

"The Wausau boys?" asked the young woman, with a confused look on her face.

"That's what we call the investigators from the Wausau Crime Lab," said Lew with a smile. "Don't ask me why. We just always have. And even though it sounds like a bunch of kids, and while some of them may be a little goofy, they are very good at what they do. We're small-town law enforcement, so it helps to have forensic experts so close at hand." Once she saw the young woman nod in understanding, Lew continued, "Your name is Diane Knutsen, right?"

"Correct."

"All right, Diane, you lead the way."

After one last check to be sure that the deputies had arrived and cordoned off the entire grounds of the camp, Lew followed Diane through a large gap in the fence behind the farthest tennis court. They headed down a narrow path that appeared little used and led up and down through the low-growing young balsam and aspen. Tree roots crossing the path proved challenging. With a loud "Whoa!" Lew tripped forward, almost losing her balance.

"Are you okay, Sheriff? This is not easy going. All my traps are set in dense brush like this." The graduate student gave a slight smile. "The grouse love it. Plenty of hiding places."

"Hold on one minute, would you please?" asked Lew, pulling her cell phone out. "And let's both of us be very careful that we don't walk on or touch anything more than we absolutely must. What I mean is that we should stay on the path just as you walked it up to the tennis courts, not veer off an inch. Also, try not to touch anything growing along the path—leaves, branches, plants, whatever—as we walk by." With that, she hit Ray's name on her phone.

"Yo, Sheriff Ferris, how are you for buttons?"

Stupefied, Lew stared at the phone for two seconds before saying, "Buttons! Buttons? What on earth? Dammit, Ray, I've got an emergency—"

"Oh, sorry. What's up?"

"Another shooting at the old camp, and this certainly is no accident. I'm standing here on a back path with a woman who says she saw someone run by with a gun. Are you familiar with the paths around here?" Before Ray could answer, she said, "Please, drop whatever you're doing. I'm deputizing you as I speak, and I need you here ASAP."

"I hear you. I'm on my way." Ray's voice was low and serious.

When Lew had ended the call, Diane said to her, "I'm not sure if it was a man or a woman." As the two of them continued down the path, Diane said, "Can I meet with the person you just talked to before they follow this path, please? I need to make sure they don't damage my grouse traps."

"Yes, I'll have you talk with Ray right after you show me where you were when you saw the person with the gun. And you don't have to worry about Ray disturbing your traps. If anything, he'll volunteer to help you." She gave Diane a smile of reassurance.

* * *

Ray Pradt was a puzzle to people familiar with his high-achieving family members. His father was a respected physician, his brother a hand surgeon, and his sister a distinguished litigator in Chicago. Ray excelled too: at fishing. While he was a sought-after fishing guide and his podcast was more popular than anyone had ever expected, his was hardly a traditional success story.

The answer lay in his childhood. When other kids signed up for soccer, Ray had devoted his summers to fishing and exploring the hemlock forest surrounding his parents' log cabin. One summer day when he was out in the old wooden rowboat that had belonged to his late uncle, he was halfway up a narrow inlet that fed into a larger lake when he saw an older Native American man who had stumbled while walking over rocks along the streambank. The old man was having trouble getting to his feet. After watching in silence for a minute or two, Ray pulled the rowboat over, jumped into the shallow stream, and waded over to the rocks to help the old man stand up.

Ray wanted to be sure no bones had been broken, so he said, "My dad's a doctor, mister. If you broke your leg, he can fix it." The old man chuckled and assured the boy he was fine. Ray wasn't sure, so he sat on a nearby log and chatted with the man until he was convinced the man was okay. And that was the start of a friendship that would change his life.

From that day on and into his late teens, Ray would hang out with the old man and close friends of his, two other older Native Americans. They taught him their secrets for catching fish, tracking deer, and trapping beaver. They taught him the secrets hidden in the sounds of the night forest: the hoots of the owls, the cries of the loons, and the screams piercing the dark.

From one of the old man's friends, he learned how to mimic the different calls of the loons, becoming so good that he could fool even the loons. "I could've married one," he once joked.

Even as he had become expert at birdcalls, he had practiced for hours trying to learn the Native Americans' methods for tracking through the forest, whether pursuing animals or humans and in all kinds of weather.

Osborne's coffee buddies liked to initiate newcomers to their early-morning gatherings at McDonald's with stories about Ray—his loon calls, his remarkable eye for tracking animals of any size through the forest. Lew didn't discount their descriptions; she knew he was that good. Better than any of the Wausau boys. And right now she needed those eyes.

* * *

At the yellow stake, Diane motioned for Lew to get down on her knees and crawl after her through the dense brush. "Be careful these branches don't hit you in the face," she said.

"Don't worry," said Lew. "I grew up in this neck of the woods. I'm very aware." Head down, she followed Diane's feet along as she crawled until they reached the long, low chicken-wire fence with the capture pen on one end. Diane explained how she would find and hold a grouse in order to band it, then use her phone to take photos of the tail feathers and the tail fan.

"So that's what I was doing when I heard the two gunshots," said Diane as she got to her feet. "I was holding the bird here"—she held her arms up to demonstrate—"when I saw the person run by. Did I mention I think I had heard them running in the direction of the tennis courts maybe ten minutes earlier?"

"No, you didn't. So they came from behind you first and then ran back and away?" Lew stood up as she talked and, looking back, said, "On the same path we were just on. Correct?"

"Yes."

"Show me again how you were standing after the gunshots."

Diane thought a moment. "So I had banded the bird and was studying the tail feathers like this"—she held both arms high—"and I was pointing my phone at the tail fan when I saw the runner coming my way." She gestured with the phone. "I could barely see the person's head over that shrub there . . ." Continuing to hold her arms and the phone high, she shifted from side to side until she was sure which way she would have been aiming while focused on the bird's tail fan.

Diane stopped talking, hit the photos icon, and stared down at her phone. "Sheriff Ferris, you won't believe this . . ." She held out the phone so Lew could see her photos. "I got it! I got pictures of that runner! I must have hit the button so hard that the phone took this entire series of shots."

Lew clicked through what had to be twenty or more shots showing a person in a blue hoodie running. Trees and brush obstructed the view below the runner's shoulders, but there was no doubt there was a figure there. The problem was the hood over the runner's head: Lew couldn't see a face.

Holding the phone, Lew said, "Diane, we have to hurry back up to the tennis courts, and I have to keep your phone until my IT person can get these photos. And I'll need your code so she can open your phone."

"Okay," said Diane, before sharing the code. "You think you'll recognize that person?"

"Once the photos are enlarged, we may be able to—I hope so."

Lew dropped to her knees, ready to crawl back to the path. Diane followed her, saying, "How long do you need my phone? I have a lot of stuff on there that I need for my research—"

"If it's going to take long, I'll make sure you have a phone you can use, but my techs are fast, so don't worry," said Lew as they reached the path and she got to her feet. Walking quickly but taking care not to stumble on the root, she looked back over her shoulder as she said, "This is critical, Diane. No one has eyes like Ray Pradt, and I need him checking this path right now before we lose whatever traces that runner may have left."

* * *

Arriving back at the tennis courts, Lew saw Osborne kneeling beside the victim, his forensic tool kit beside him. "I'll take care of the death certificate, Lew," he said without looking up from the still figure. "She's been shot twice. I'll let the pathologist at the crime lab determine which bullet killed her, but I've no doubt it's the one she took in the back of the head. I can also see that she has two exit wounds. Between the Wausau boys and Ray, someone should be able to find the spent shells. Poor woman."

He got to his feet and looked at Lew. "Based on what I see, she didn't know what hit her—died instantly."

"I'm here, Lew," said a low voice from behind her. "Another accident?"

Lew shook her head. "No. And not only that, but Diane here nearly witnessed it." She gestured with one hand as she turned toward the young woman. "Ray, this is Diane Knutsen. She's a grad student researching ruffed grouse. I'll let her tell you more, but what's critical right now is that she was down the path that runs behind these courts—"

"I know the path," said Ray.

"Good. She was checking one of her traps she uses to band the birds when she heard gunshots and a moment later saw someone run by carrying a rifle."

"Got it," said Ray. Turning to Diane, Ray reached out to shake hands. "Diane? Nice meeting you. I'm Ray Pradt, and as you can see, I work for Sheriff Ferris here. If you're ready, let's go right now and have you show me where you were when you heard the gunshots. I should be able to take it from there."

*　*　*

With that, the two started walking toward the back of the tennis courts. They made an odd pair. Ray had to be at least a foot taller than the young woman, who walked with her shoulders hunched, her head down. Determined. Ray's shoulders were hunched too as he leaned over to hear what she was saying.

Lew was relieved that for once he had held his often inappropriate humor in check. She was especially happy that he hadn't shown up wearing his hat with the stuffed trout fixed between his ears. Though he was wearing that sweatshirt of his, the one emblazoned with *FISHING WITH RAY: Excitement, Romance and Live Bait*. Lew shrugged; that was a small irritation. It was obvious Ray understood today was a day to be dead serious—a day when one woman had ended up dead.

"Hold on, Ray," said Osborne, calling out just as Ray was holding the torn wire fencing back so Diane could walk through the gap easily. "Please be sure to stop back here when you can."

Osborne got to his feet and pointed toward the body of Robin Carpenter. "This victim has been shot twice and has two exit wounds. You know what that means: we might be able to find the bullet that killed her. Or you might—"

"Doc's right," said Lew, calling out in a loud voice to be sure Ray could hear her. "Bruce and a couple of the Wausau boys will be here shortly, but we all know you have eyes they don't."

Just then Lew remembered cutting him off earlier. "Oh, and sorry, I almost forgot to ask. What was that you mentioned about buttons?" Lew remembered being brusque with him on the phone and couldn't help feeling guilty, in spite of her need at the time to get Diane's phone to Dani, whose IT skills might be able to identify the suspect. Two seconds of thoughtfulness couldn't have hurt.

"Yeah, right. I need buttons if you have any," said Ray, before following Diane through the fence. "You know, my worm harness?"

"Yes?"

"It keeps snagging on the lake bottom. I figure if I tie on a tiny button, that might stop the snagging." His eyes brightened as he called back to her, "Worth six bluegills, doncha know."

"Got it," said Lew, managing a laugh. "I'll check my sewing basket. Used to do a lot of sewing when my kids were growing up. I'm sure I've got something for you."

With a wave, Ray and Diane disappeared behind the ragged wire fence and headed down the path. Watching them go, Lew couldn't help but wonder if this unexpected meeting of the two might not be serendipitous. They were both young and single and both addicted to nature in their own unique ways.

She turned to Osborne, who asked, "What are you thinking, Lewellyn? You look so serious."

"Not thinking, just speculating."

"Well, I brought you a mug of hot coffee. It's in my car. If you wish, we can wait there for the Wausau boys."

"Thanks, Doc. Yes, sounds good, but I have to drink fast. Diane had her phone up and was taking photos of the bird's tail feathers in the direction of that path right when the shooter ran by. There's a series of shots on this"—she held up Diane's phone—"and I've got to get it to Dani as soon as I can."

As they walked quickly toward Osborne's car, Lew reached for her cell phone. "Excuse me, Doc, while I call Dani. I need her to cancel any IT requests on her desk until we can download these photos. Then I'd love a few sips of coffee, but I've got to head into town. Will you wait for Bruce? He should arrive any moment. Tell him what you've found?"

"Yes, I will, and I'm not sure you need coffee, Lewellyn. You're wound pretty tight already."

Lew gave Doc a wry grin as they hurried past the crime scene tape the deputies had put up around the old tennis courts.

Chapter Sixteen

Lew was still talking to Dani as she climbed into the passenger seat of Osborne's Subaru and watched as he poured her a mug of hot coffee from his thermos. The second she was off her phone, there was a knocking on her window. She turned to see three faces staring at her.

Recognizing the three pickleball players who had driven up right behind her earlier, she lowered the window to let them know she had no official news yet. But she hadn't even opened her mouth when the man standing closest to the window said, "Sheriff Ferris, we're pretty sure we know who shot poor Robin—"

The man was so tense, his shoulders were shaking. He wasn't alone in his anxiety. The two people with him were so wired they gave the impression of jumping up and down.

"Okay, okay, settle down. I'm getting out of the car to talk to you guys," said Lew as she set her coffee mug into the cupholder and opened the car door.

"Yeah, he was so mad he was spitting," said a woman who had elbowed her way in front of the man with the vibrating shoulders.

"And you are?" asked Lew, interrupting her.

"Rosie Heston. I'm Clyde Moore's partner." She pointed at the man who had knocked on the window. "We're the number-two team behind Bert and Robin. Well, we were, and this is Terry Craft. He's going to, oh, he was going to play Bert's position, but . . ."

"I see. Now what's this about someone spitting? And, people, I only have a minute or two. I have to rush some evidence to my office. So I'm sorry, but you have to talk fast."

"Let me," said Clyde, pushing his partner out of the way. "See, Bert bought this place last spring so we'd have a good hiding place to practice. At the time, that A-frame next door was still under construction. Idiot didn't move in until August, and then he started bugging us.

"Now, we like to practice at six thirty in the morning, 'cause I still work full-time. So that jerk moves into his new place and starts coming over to holler that the sound of our balls was waking him up. He must have shouted at us to stop playing, what"—Clyde looked at his friends for their opinions—"maybe six or seven times?"

"At least. Maybe more," said Rosie, so upset she was continuing to bounce on her toes.

"This last time—the day before Bert was shot—that guy was over here like Rumpelstiltskin, jumping up and down, he was so angry with us. He bothered us so much that morning we couldn't play. We quit early."

"I kid you not," said Rosie. "He marched up to me and shouted right in my face, spit at me. Literally. I'm not making that up. I had to wipe his spit off my cheek."

"And who is this man?" asked Lew.

"Larry. Larry Weston, and he lives right there." All three pointed to a brand-new A-frame style house farther down the dirt road and about two hundred yards from the entrance to the boys' camp.

"Okay," said Lew. "Thank you for your information. I will question him."

"Right now." This came from Clyde and sounded like a demand.

Knowing they were upset, Lew stayed calm. "There are legal protocols I have to follow, and if you are correct, which you may be, I need a search warrant. I will be driving to my office right now to get that warrant."

"Should we wait here?" asked Rosie.

"No, please, I need all three of you to leave. The Wausau Crime Lab investigating team is arriving any moment, and they need to clear the area. I will be back to question Mr. Weston shortly."

"Will you let us know if you arrest him?"

"Yes. You may call Judith Hanson at the McBride County Sheriff's Department. She is my admin, and she will have all the information. So thank you."

With that, Lew got back in Osborne's car and, desperate for a shot of caffeine, reached for the coffee mug. After swallowing, she turned to Osborne, who had been listening, and asked, "Do you know this guy? Larry Weston?"

"Never heard of him. But I'll stop by the Loon Lake Bar and see if anyone is familiar with the guy."

* * *

It was a little after eight thirty when Deb got back from picking up Jane's groceries. Thursday was the day the Loon Lake Market put their Cleary's ice cream on sale, a popular one-day sale, and Jane insisted Deb be in line to get her three pints of mint chocolate chip ice cream. Three pints would last her a week, and then Deb would be in line again. Deb didn't mind, as she did her own grocery shopping too and charged Jane for her time.

After unloading the ice cream and other grocery items, Deb walked up to the front door to see if the mail had arrived. She picked up two envelopes and a magazine, which she put on the side table by the stairwell in the front hall. She sensed that finding the mail set out on the small table at the bottom of the elegant winding oak staircase made Jane feel like she had a household staff: maids and servants and footmen. Whatever. As long as Deb was getting paid, she didn't mind doing it.

Glancing into the room holding Bert's gun collection, she noticed the Browning rifle had been returned. She wasn't surprised. Robin Steadman must have returned it on her way to the dental office, though Deb had thought the office was closed until after Jane was able to arrange Bert's funeral. She shrugged and walked back to the kitchen, noticing as she went that the front hallway needed a good mopping.

* * *

Lew didn't get to her office until shortly after nine. Judith and Dani crowded around her as she held up Diane Knutsen's iPhone to show them the series of photos Diane had shot of the person with the rifle.

"I can't make out the face. Can you?" Judith asked Lew and Dani. "My eyesight isn't great."

"I can't either," said Lew. She turned to Dani, asking, "Can you?"

"No, that hoodie is covering the features. You've got the phone code, right?"

"Yes," said Lew, handing her the piece of paper where Diane had written it. "How long will it take for you to get the photos off here? Diane needs her phone back right away for her research."

"Shouldn't take long," said Dani. "I'll email those to myself, and then I should be able to enlarge them. I'd like to keep the phone until I know I can work with the photos. Okay?"

"Should be fine. I have three people who arrived at the scene this morning right after Robin Carpenter was shot. They insist the shooter is a guy living nearby, so I have to get back out there. I promised them I would question the man."

"Sounds like you don't believe them," said Judith.

Lew sighed. "I don't know. I find it less than plausible that someone could be so angry about people playing ball in their backyard. But we'll see. Nuts are everywhere."

"And that widow I told you about," said Judith, getting to her feet. "Don't forget her, Lew. In my opinion, she had good cause to hate Bert. The person who alerted me said the widow has been quite depressed and uncommunicative. Friends of hers are worried she might do something extreme."

Lew gave Judith a long look. "I will definitely talk to her, but while I can see her angry with Bert Willoughby, why would she attack the woman? Doesn't make sense. Though I am beginning to think that Bert's death was not an accident."

Dani had started to leave the office, Diane's phone in her hand, when Lew said, "Dani, I have an odd question. When I deputized Ray to help with the investigation this morning, he asked me if I have any buttons for his worm harness. Are you helping him with that?"

"No," said Dani, "and I hope this doesn't hurt your feelings, because I know he's one of your close friends, but no. We're better off buddies, Sheriff. And"—she squinted as if embarrassed to mention it—"I got a new guy. And, well, we're pretty serious. Ray is wonderful, but . . ."

* * *

After walking up the stairway and down the hall to the dental offices, Robin Steadman was alarmed to find the office door unlocked. Had someone broken in? "Hello-o-o-o?" she called out in a wary tone.

"Just me," hollered a voice back. It was Katherine.

"Oh, thank goodness," said Robin, relieved. "I was worried."

"Well, don't be," said Katherine as she walked out of the small room farther down the hallway that served as her office. "I can only take so much of Mom in the morning." She laughed. "And I've promised to stay over at her place one more night, so I need a break. Since the office is closed until next week—at least I assume we'll be able to hold Dad's funeral next week—I thought I would catch up with my patient charts. Did you tell me the new owner of Dad's practice takes over in four months? Or is it five?"

"Pretty sure it's four," said Robin. "I feel so bad he didn't tell you about that."

"Hey, it's a gift, frankly. A classmate of mine from dental school reached out to me just last week. She's setting up a new practice in Wausau and was hoping to recruit me. She's aiming to make it the first all-female practice in Wisconsin. Isn't that cool?"

"Wow," said Robin. "That makes me feel better about everything. Talk about timing. That's terrific. Please be sure to let me know whatever you need, but this gives both of us time to prepare the patients, get the office ready, everything. I need a little good news, and this makes my day, Katherine."

"Robin, I apologize again for my mother's behavior. She was pretty wonky after losing Dad, but there was no excuse for that."

"I understand," said Robin, setting her purse down and pulling out the chair at the receptionist's desk. "I'm working on billing, so if you need anything. When I finish here, I'll be in the lab. We have some impressions I need to take care of."

"Don't think so. I just finished updating the charts." Katherine gave Robin a friendly grimace as she said, "Been here since before seven, so it feels like a long day already. I'm going to go through Dad's office too. Let you know if I have any questions."

"You'll need the key to his desk," said Robin, bending over to reach into her purse, which she had just stuffed into the bottom desk drawer. She held the key out to Katherine. "You can keep it if you wish. I never go into his desk. And let me know if you can't get into his computer."

"Thank you. I will. My mother may want to visit his office too." She smiled at Robin and turned to walk toward the large room at the back of the offices that had been her father's office.

Once there, she pushed open the folding doors to check out his closet. Two of the white jackets he'd worn while treating patients were hanging there, still in plastic from the cleaners, along with an old winter jacket. On the floor was a pair of scruffy slippers. She closed the closet and walked over to her dad's desk.

She had no interest in the computer but was curious as to why her father would have locked his desk. She tried the drawer. Locked. She inserted the key and opened the drawer. At the front were several pens, paper clips, and a nail file. Behind the section holding the pens were two stacks of twenty-, fifty-, and hundred-dollar bills. Stunned at the sight of the money, Katherine fingered the stacks, estimating she was looking at ten thousand dollars or more. She stared at it a few seconds, then closed and locked the drawer.

She walked into the lab, where Robin, in an apron, was busy with impressions. "I opened my dad's desk drawer, and he had some cash in there. Do you know why? I mean, don't patients use insurance or pay the receptionist? Why would my dad have cash?"

"He had cash in the drawer?" said Robin, surprised. "I had no idea. But now that you mention it, one of his patients complained to me that your dad charged too much. I told your dad about the patient, and he made the guy a deal—if the patient paid him in cash, he would give him a discount. Maybe that's what the money's for. But I'm not sure. Your father and I never talked about the office finances aside from the recordkeeping for billing patients."

"I see," said Katherine. She walked back into her father's office and opened the drawer with the cash. She reached to grab the money, only to pause. All she had on was a black turtleneck and a pair of black joggers that had only a small pocket for keys. *No purse—darn.* She checked around the room, hoping to find a pouch or bag of some kind; maybe one of her dad's jackets she could wrap it in? No luck. She would have to come back for the money.

With a shrug, she decided to take a few minutes and open the remaining drawers in his desk. She found a monthly accounting book. Opening it, she found a list of people's initials alongside a list of cash payments. As she studied the list and the amounts, she began to see a pattern: if a patient paid in cash, Bert would charge half the amount he had requested.

Next, Katherine asked herself the obvious: Did Dr. Bert Willoughby not report his cash earnings? The man she knew as her father had been so stingy with money—except when it came to his gun collection—that she'd bet he cheated on his taxes.

Well, why not? she thought. If you're going to cheat your wife and your daughter, why not cheat the federal government?

Chapter Seventeen

As Lew drove in the directions of the old boys' camp and the tennis courts, her cell phone rang. She glanced down to see Bruce Peters's name. "Hey, Bruce," she said as she answered.

"Sheriff, that young woman, Diane, just ran back and asked me to let you know that Ray found cartridges that may have been dropped by the individual she saw running with the rifle."

"You're kidding—we mean we caught a break?" said Lew. "I'll be there shortly, but unless you think this requires me being there immediately, I need to catch up with someone first."

"No rush," said Bruce. "I'm sure we'll be here all day."

* * *

In spite of the accusations made by the three pickleball players, Lew found it hard to believe that the owner of the new A-frame—angry though he might be about the early-morning *pop-pop* of pickleballs—would be so foolish as to shoot at the players. He might *want* to, but wanting and doing were nowhere near the same.

Nevertheless, she needed to hear the neighbor, Larry Weston, confirm that he had done nothing so foolish. And just in case there was something out of whack with the guy, she had made sure to have warrants in hand so she could demonstrate to the trio that she had listened to their allegations and was prepared to validate them. And now was the time to prove they were wrong, so she and the Wausau boys could continue working their investigation without interruptions.

After pulling onto the unfinished driveway running along one side of the contemporary-style new house, she found a newly paved walkway leading to three stone steps. At the top of the steps, she crossed unpainted wood flooring and peered through two wide glass front doors. On a wood panel to the left of the doors, a colorful ceramic owl perched, holding a black button in its beak.

After pressing the button, Lew leaned forward, trying to see into the darkened interior of the house. Just beyond the entryway, she could make out a dining area fronted by an elevated counter with matching chairs, likely a bar. She waited. She pressed the button again.

Though she could hear the doorbell ringing, no one appeared. Nor did any lights come on inside the house. She hadn't seen a car parked in the drive, but there might be a garage on the lower level behind the house. She was about to check on that when she saw movement out of the corner of her eye. Or thought she saw movement . . .

Lew stepped closer to the glass doors, her face almost touching the glass, and looked in, waiting. Looking up and past the dining area, she could see a reflection in the wide plate-glass window on the far wall: Someone was on their knees, hiding behind the counter. She knocked hard on the glass door. The figure didn't move.

"I see you, Mr. Weston," she said, raising her voice. "I'm Sheriff Lewellyn Ferris, and you need to open this door immediately. Stand up. Now. And open this door."

Lew pulled out her Sig Sauer semiautomatic pistol and turned sideways to the doorframe, watching. She prayed the man wasn't armed and about to do something stupid. She spoke again: "Lawrence Weston, I have a search warrant, and if you do not respond to my instructions, you will be placed under arrest."

The figure appeared to hesitate, then scrambled to its feet. The man walked over to the door, a sheepish look on his face. He unlocked the door.

"I understand, and I apologize," he said. He was short and wiry, with a buzz cut of sandy hair standing on end across his skull. Lew guessed him to be in his forties. "I thought you were one of those pickleball nuts—"

"Really?" said Lew. "What is it about a uniform, a badge, and a gun that makes you think pickleball?" She wasn't being funny, but the man seemed genuinely contrite.

"I was crouching and couldn't see you," he said earnestly. "If I had seen your badge, Sheriff Ferris, I would certainly have come to the door, but I had my head down, so I couldn't see. They've been calling me, heckling me, leaving nasty notes in my mailbox. Those people are horrible." He stepped back as he talked, holding the door open for Lew to enter the house. "I am so sorry. I overreacted, I know." Lew could hear the anxiety in his voce.

"I need your gun—all your guns."

"I don't have a gun. I don't own a gun. I'm not a hunter—I fish."

After putting away her Sig Sauer, Lew pulled out her cell phone and called her office. "Dani, please check to see if there are any firearms registered to a Larry—or Lawrence—Weston . . . Good, I'll wait." She kept her eyes on the man in front of her as she said, "Stand right there until I tell you to move."

The guy raised both hands. "Please, I promise. I won't move, and I am so sorry—"

Lew waved for him to stop talking, then spoke again into her phone. "Good. Thank you, Dani, that's all I need for the moment."

Lew continued to study the man standing in front of her. After a long minute, she said, "I believe you, Mr. Weston. I'm not going to arrest you. Can you tell me why you have been so angry with those people playing a sport over at the old boys' camp? I mean, what if that camp was still open and full of young kids? With all that noise? What would you do then?"

"I wouldn't have bought this goddamn property. I wouldn't have built this goddamn house."

"That makes sense," said Lew with a slight smile. "But you've built a home in an area that gets a lot of boat and summer tourist traffic. You will have noise. I'm not sure they won't play pickleball next door again someday. You can't be threatening people for making harmless noises."

"I understand," said Weston, shaking his head and looking humble. "I promise, Sheriff, it won't happen again."

Lew started to walk out the door, then paused and turned back, saying, "You may not know this yet, but there was a shooting at the tennis courts this morning. Did you hear gunshots?"

"No, but I was on the lake at five. I didn't get back here until half an hour ago, but I sure see all the cop cars and the ambulance over there. Who got shot?"

"One of the pickleball players," said Lew.

"Oh my gosh. One of the players got that mad?"

"No. Had to be someone standing outside the tennis courts. I'm wondering if you've seen anyone lurking around there? I realize there's a couple hundred yards between your place and the entrance to the old camp, but maybe you've seen someone? Unfamiliar cars parking nearby?"

"No, only the same cars that have been parking there all summer," he said. "You know who I mean—the jerk who owns the place and his friends."

Lew ignored the man's remark. He would hear about Bert's death soon enough. Instead she asked, "So no cars driving past your place and further down that dirt road?"

"No, and I would notice if they did. A major reason I bought this land is because that road is a dead end. Used to be a logging road led to an old cabin down at the end of that point behind me, on the shore looking over the

channel between the lakes. But when I bought the land—
and I own this entire peninsula, from the camp property
line west to the water—I tore the old cabin down and put
up a NO TRESPASSING sign. And just so you know, the shoreline there is so rocky that no kids or anybody tries to pull
up a boat to fish there either. So, no, I haven't seen anyone."
He paused. "Does that help?"

"I hope so," said Lew. "You say you were on the lake at
five this morning?"

"Yes, but I like to be out there earlier, like by four thirty.
I like to fish early, come back, and take a nap, then go out
again. That's why the pickleball players are so irritating—
they mess up my nap."

"What are you catching so early in the morning?" Lew
was curious. She didn't know many fishermen who liked to
go out before dawn.

"Walleyes. Love 'em. I use a worm harness, and wham!
You wouldn't believe how well that works."

"Oh, I do. A good friend recently showed me his. His
name is Ray Pradt—ever heard of him?" Lew could see the
man calming down as she chatted with him. Hopefully,
he'd stay calm.

"Sure have. Listen to his podcast every week. He's the
expert. Do you fish?" asked Weston.

"I fly-fish."

"Oh." His disappointment was obvious.

"I'm curious," said Lew, hoping to keep him talking a
few minutes longer. "You have a unique property here. Was
it your family's?"

"Gosh, no. I'm from Chicago, but my folks sent me to summer camp up in Eagle River. One of the counselors there was from Rhinelander and told me about the walleyes in Loon Lake. Five years ago, when I made some money in the stock market, I started keeping an eye out for properties in this area—and lucked out one day when I saw the peninsula for sale. Got it for a song." Weston gave Lew a broad grin, which told her he was in much better humor.

"You did indeed luck out," said Lew. "The dark water in this chain means no or very little invasive species, so shoreline values are skyrocketing." Lew reached out to shake his hand. "Mr. Weston, you are one smart walleye guy. Now, be kind to the pickleballers, okay?"

"I promise," said Weston with a sheepish look on his face. "I do, really."

Minutes later, Lew walked back to her cruiser, still wondering what kind of forty-year-old got down on his knees to hide behind a counter instead of answering his front door. What a razzbonya.

*　*　*

Back at the tennis courts, Lew caught up with Bruce, who was in conversation with Diane. When they saw Lew approaching, Bruce held up an evidence bag as he said, "Here they are, Lew—three cartridges the shooter dropped."

"Yes, Sheriff Ferris," said Diane. "Now I know what happened when I saw that person running back down the path. I remember how I thought for a moment that the runner had seen me and was coming toward where I was standing by my grouse trap, but what they were really doing was trying to find the cartridges they dropped. Thank goodness. I was terrified."

"Think we can get fingerprints?" Lew asked Bruce.

"Pretty sure. I'm sending these down to our lab in a few minutes so we'll be able to run a check late today."

Turning to the young woman standing with Bruce, Lew said, "Diane, we should be able to return your phone to you this afternoon. Dani, who handles IT for us, wanted to keep it until she could be sure she can work with the photos okay."

"Oh, not to worry, Sheriff. I already have my phone," said Diane, holding it up. "One of your deputies drove it out here half an hour ago. Works fine too."

"Good. Now, I'm sure at least six people have asked you this, Diane, but I will anyway. I know you've been checking your grouse traps, and I know they're in different locations, but I have a question regarding this one. When you've been here checking your trap, have you noticed other cars parked down that lane where you parked this morning?"

"Not this morning, for sure," said Diane. "Ray asked me that right away. And, no, never when I've been checking. It's a dead end, so no reason for anyone to drive it. That's why I thought the person I saw was a runner who knew the path and wanted to keep off Loon Lake Road, because there's no bike lane and too many curves."

"Okay. Just checking," said Lew with a nod.

"You're only the third person to ask me," Diane said with a slight smile. Lew could tell she was still trying to relax after what she'd been through that morning. "Bruce told me you teach fly-fishing—and you're an expert. I've always wanted to learn."

"Ray overheard me telling her about you," said Bruce, who had been standing nearby listening, "and he's offered to teach her how to fish muskies."

"I want to learn both," said Diane. Lew could see her spirits lifting by the moment.

"Okay," said Lew, "but first I have to find who killed that poor woman this morning. Then we can talk." Diane's face fell enough for Lew to pause and say, "I'm impressed with the research you're doing on grouse, so not to worry, Diane, I'll try to find time to get you started before the trout season ends."

"I may have to come along and watch," said Bruce, eyebrows bouncing. "I need every tip I can get."

Chapter Eighteen

Lew made a quick dash home to her farmhouse, where she could grab a quick lunch but, more important, a small cloth bag from her sewing kit. Ray needed buttons, and if there was one thing she had plenty of, it was buttons.

She had buttons she had inherited from her grandmother and her mother. The buttons had served her well as a parent and a grandparent, and now they might save the podcast career of a talented muskie fisherman. Who knew? Life took strange turns.

Laying the precious bag of buttons on the passenger seat of her cruiser, Lew buckled in and headed back to her office and the search for Robin Carpenter's killer.

* * *

It was two in the afternoon when Lew lifted the brass knocker on the front door of the home belonging to the wife of the late George Patterson, the man who'd died after Bert Willoughby failed to diagnose the cancer of the tongue that metastasized and killed him. The tall two-story home was unique in Loon Lake. Beige stucco walls held three large front windows set side by side and bordered with forest-green wooden shutters. At the sound of the brass knocker, the dark-red oak door to the right of the windows opened.

Lew stepped back, almost knocking Osborne off the stoop where he stood waiting behind her. "Oops, sorry, Doc," she said, grabbing his arm.

"I apologize for the narrow stoop there," said the woman who had opened the door. "George was planning to have that redone. Too many people have stumbled and fallen. Sheriff Ferris? Please, come in. I'm Lindsey Patterson."

She extended her hand with a slight smile, though Lew was struck by the darkness in her eyes. She might have been determined to look pleased to see them, but it was a futile effort.

"And you are?" The woman looked at Osborne.

"Dr. Paul Osborne," said Osborne, reaching to shake her hand. "Sheriff Ferris asked me to come along, as I'm a retired dentist and I understand some of the issues you and your husband had to deal with during his illness."

"Really?" She gave him a doubtful look. "I don't think anyone can."

"Dr. Osborne is also the McBride County acting coroner," said Lew. "He's a member of my law enforcement team."

"I see." Lindsey had turned and walked into the living room, which was just inside the front hall. "Please sit down. I know why you're here, and I assure you I'm willing to answer all your questions. But . . . much as I hate that man, I assure you I did not shoot him."

"Oh—" Lew was taken aback by her bluntness.

"I'm not stupid," said the widow. "If you made a list of everyone who wanted Bert Willoughby dead, I would be at the top. And for good reason. Sit down, both of you." She gestured toward a long sofa that sat in front of the three windows.

Bitter though the woman sounded, she had an edge to her that Lew liked. Lew couldn't help thinking this was someone she would like to know better, someone she would like to know as a friend someday when the woman's grief and anger weren't quite so intense.

Hoping to relieve a little of the pressure of the moment, Lew glanced around the room before saying, "This is an extraordinary house. Beautiful."

"Thank you. My husband was a professor of architecture at the university, so when we decided to retire here, we were pleased to find this house. It's one of three in this area that were designed by a student of Frank Lloyd Wright."

"I did not know that," said Osborne, looking around the room. "I do know that a close friend of my father's lived here. He was a doctor, so I was here once or twice when I was growing up. There was a baby grand piano in that corner," said Osborne, pointing to his left.

His remarks seemed to relax Lindsey a little. "This house meant a lot to my husband. He loved it so much, the only changes he would let me make were to repaint the walls in the kitchen and our bedroom . . ."

Before she could finish, tears were spilling down her cheeks. "Sorry," she said, wiping her face with a Kleenex. "This keeps happening when I least expect it—so sorry."

"Please, don't worry," said Lew. "Dr. Osborne and I understand. But, Lindsey, I do have to ask you several questions. My first is, do you have guns in the house?"

"Of course," said Lindsey, taking a deep breath as she finished wiping at her cheeks. "George and I loved to hunt grouse, and we enjoyed shooting trap too. I'm sure you'd like to see the guns, so please come with me."

With that, she got to her feet and walked back toward the front hall. Once in the hall, she motioned for them to follow her down the hall and past a small kitchen, where she said with a chuckle, "This was built in the day when everyone had a cook. If I'd had my way, I would have doubled the size of this room."

After a quick glance around, Lew and Osborne followed her into a back room. Clothes hooks ran along the right wall, and a rack of shotguns occupied the left.

"Here they are," said Lindsey with a wave of her hand. "And if you need to take any for testing, I don't mind, but I do want them back."

"No, not necessary," said Lew. "I'm looking for a particular Browning rifle."

"You need to see this too," said Lindsey, pulling open a drawer below the gun rack and reaching for a pistol. She held it up and away as she said, "This is a .22 pistol I've owned since I was twelve years old. Two days after George's funeral, I put it in my purse, drove to the Willoughby dental office, parked my car . . . sat there. And I cried."

Lew and Osborne stood silent. Neither spoke.

Lindsey put the pistol back in the drawer and shut it. "I wanted to kill the son of a bitch. I couldn't do it." She managed a feeble grin. "I know I told a couple of my women friends I was going to do it. That's why you're here, right?"

Lew nodded.

"Let's go back to your living room and talk," said Osborne.

The three of them walked back down the hallway, past the kitchen, to the living room, where they sat down. "I understand you filed a malpractice lawsuit and lost, correct?" asked Osborne.

"Yes. I filed when we were told George's tongue cancer was terminal, but the lawsuit was dismissed."

"I'm not surprised. Unless the patient is deceased, it is very difficult to win a medical malpractice case in Wisconsin. You might try again," said Osborne. "If you wish, I can recommend an oral surgeon to review your husband's medical records."

"I would appreciate that," said Lindsey, sounding grateful. "Losing George this way has been so unfair. I would like to give a lawsuit one more try, especially as I know Bert Willoughby was worth a lot of money."

"I don't know that it helps at all for me to say this," said Osborne, "but you're not alone in your feelings of anger and loss and frustration. Bert Willoughby let many people down in ways that have proved devastating. I am so sorry this had to happen to you and George. If you would give me your phone number, I'll call you with the name and contact information for my friend who is an excellent oral surgeon. Yours will not be the first case like this that he's reviewed. Who knows? He may find something that can lead to settlement, though of course it won't bring back your husband."

"I so appreciate that," said Lindsey, grasping Osborne's hand. "I'm determined to make one last try."

Lew started toward the front door. "This has been very helpful, Lindsey. I appreciate your frankness, and I am so sorry for your loss. Thank you for taking time with us today."

After following them to the door, Lindsey looked over at Lew and said, "You know, Sheriff Ferris, my women friends have made one remark that I'd like to share, though I know it's rather mean-spirited."

"Go right ahead," said Lew, stepping out onto the stoop. "I appreciate what you've shared with me so far."

"Well, it seems that Bert Willoughby was quite the man about town. He had more than a few 'ladies on the side,' as my friends say—and they think that Jane may have hired a hit man."

"Whoa, that's a thought," said Osborne.

Lew, taken aback, was speechless for a long minute before she managed to say, "I can see the reasoning. I'll keep that in mind."

Minutes later, sitting in her cruiser, Lew turned to Osborne and said, "My list of people who had it in for Bert Willoughby is growing. Now I have Jane's hit man."

"That is not as absurd as it sounds," said Osborne with a shake of his head. "Not at all."

Chapter Nineteen

～

When Lew walked into her office, she found Judith waiting impatiently. She hadn't even reached her desk before Judith said, "Good timing, Lew. I have good news and better news. I just had a call from Bruce Peters, who said that one of the Wausau boys may have found one of the bullets they believe killed Robin Carpenter. Ray Pradt found one too. Bruce said to let you know both bullets are on the way to the lab along with the cartridges Ray found earlier."

As Lew settled into her desk chair, Judith added, "No, don't sit down. Come with me. Dani wants to show us the photos she downloaded from Diane Knutsen's phone. She's got them up on her largest screen, and she has a theory that she wants to share—but only after you and I take a look and make our own judgments."

"Great," said Lew. "I've been thinking about those photos and whether or not we might see something that'll help with the investigation. I've ruled out two of our hot tips so far, which doesn't surprise me."

"Nor me," said Judith, "but there's an emergency situation you may need to deal with first. It's not related to our investigation, but it's troubling."

"Tell me about it," said Lew as they walked down the hall toward Dani's conference room. "Something personal?"

"For you, not me," said Judith. "One of your daughter Suzanne's close friends called about an hour ago. Her name is DeeDee—"

"Sure, I know DeeDee," said Lew. "I consider her my second daughter. I know her kids and her husband. No one's sick, I hope."

"Not that," said Judith. "She called to say there's a boy in their neighborhood with a gun, and he's been goofing off and shooting it around the kids—"

Lew stopped to stare at Judith. "Are you kidding me? They live out near Doc's place on one of the side roads. Those kids are only nine, ten years old. How long ago did she call?" Lew reached for her cell phone.

"Here's her number," said Judith, handing over a notepad. "She's at home and waiting to hear from you."

Lew punched in the number. The familiar voice answered immediately. "DeeDee, what is this?" Lew asked. She listened, then said, "I'll be there in thirty minutes. Have the kids stay indoors until I get there—okay? And DeeDee, I'll take care of this kid and his gun, so try to take it easy if you can."

Her phone off, Lew looked at Judith. "The woman's really frightened," she said.

"That's why I knew I better tell you right away."

"Let's take a quick look at Dani's photos, then I'm out of here."

The two women ran into the conference room, where Dani was waiting. Diane's camera had shot sixteen photos in rapid succession showing the figure running a short distance. Leaning forward to study each enlarged shot, Lew could make out only the hooded figure, face covered. Tree branches, pine needles, and dense brush obscured everything below shoulder level.

"I don't know," said Lew to Dani. "I can't make out anything except that blue hoodie, dammit."

Shaking her head, Judith said, "Sorry, me too. Darn."

"Yes, but a *blue* hoodie, right?" asked Dani, brushing her long, wavy curls back behind her ears. "What shade of blue?"

"Bright blue," said Lew.

"Kind of blue green, maybe?" Judith's voice rose on the end of her question.

"*Electric* blue," said Dani. Her tone implied she was teaching them the Ten Commandments.

"Well, you're the fashionista," said Lew, who would never forget the effort it had taken to lure Dani from her life goal of running a beauty salon over to helping Lew and the Loon Lake Police solve a case with IT, a field in which she'd proved to be a natural talent.

"Electric blue? How 'bout ultramarine?" asked Judith, half kidding. "I mean, blue is blue, right?"

"No it is not. That color, for example," said Dani, pointing at the screen, "is closer to cerulean."

"Cerulean? Never heard of that," said Judith.

"How about plain old bright blue?" said Lew, getting to her feet. "And I have to get out of here. You two can argue."

"You're missing the point, Sheriff Ferris," said Dani with a smirk.

"Guess I am. What's the point?" asked Lew.

"Think about who would wear a hoodie that color." Dani sat back, a triumphant smile on her face.

Lew returned to her chair and stared at the screen. "You know . . . I think you're right. We're probably looking at a woman up there."

"You think?" Judith sounded skeptical.

"I don't *think*," said Dani. "I've been in the beauty business since I was in middle school. Trust me, I know what colors people go for this time of year. Most of the men around here are pretty conservative—ninety-nine percent of the time, they go for black or navy blue."

* * *

Eight minutes later, Lew found herself making a left turn off Loon Lake Road and onto Pelican Place, a street leading into a neighborhood of modest ranch houses, many with bikes and trikes strewn across their driveways. The wide paved street along with a nearby public beach made it an ideal neighborhood for young families.

It had been a while since Lew had seen her daughter's best friend, but she knew DeeDee had at least two young children. When she reached the address DeeDee had left with Judith, she swung into the driveway in front of a two-car garage, parked, and hurried up a paved walkway to the front door.

"Oh, thank goodness, Mrs. Ferris," said the young woman who opened the door before Lew could ring the doorbell.

Dolores "DeeDee" Burns was as round faced and ash blond as she had been in her teens, maybe a touch heavier, but her blue eyes were bright as ever. Just the sight of her made Lew feel good. DeeDee had been a stalwart friend to her daughter, Suzanne, when Lew was going through a difficult divorce and had lost her son in a bar fight.

"Come in and meet my kids," said DeeDee, pulling at Lew while pushing her son and daughter forward. "Jamie is nine, and Jeff is almost eleven. They saw the bullet and the gun—"

"Okay, slow down," said Lew, following DeeDee and the two kids into their living room. It was a large room with a long, angled sofa and two upholstered chairs in front of a wide-screen television. Behind the sofa was a large picture window facing east.

"Start at the beginning," said Lew as she took a seat on one of the chairs across from the family.

Jamie, the daughter, spoke first. "This boy, Danny, is new on our street. He lives down the road with his dad. He keeps coming over and wants to do stuff with us, but last week he brought a gun, so we told him we had to go somewhere. Kinda scared me, even though Jeff thought the gun was fake."

"Then . . . ," DeeDee urged her daughter. "Then what happened this morning?"

"Well, this morning, he came over again, but this time he wanted to show us how he could shoot. So he went next door and turned around real fast to shoot at the car across the street. Like he was on TV or something."

"Oh," said Lew, getting to her feet. "You're serious? Did he hit the car? Was someone in it?"

"That's when I called your office," said DeeDee. "Come outside. I'll show you what he hit. But, no, he didn't hit the car, thank heavens. At least he hasn't yet."

They all got up and rushed out the front door into the yard. DeeDee walked over to a young oak tree growing near the street. She reached out to point to a spot on the trunk of the tree. "Here, Mrs. Ferris. Right here is what he hit."

"Mom, she's the sheriff," said Jeff, sounding reluctant but determined to correct his mother.

"Oh, I'm sorry, Sheriff—see this? It's a bullet hole, and you can feel the bullet in there. A real bullet! That boy is shooting around my kids," said DeeDee, hysteria crowding into her voice.

Lew reached up to touch the spot. "You're right, DeeDee. Do we know where the boy is now?"

"Yes," she said, pointing down the block. "The house on the corner. He's there with his dad. But let us show you what he did earlier this week first. C'mon around the house."

Lew ran behind the three to their backyard, where she saw a small wooden tree house about ten feet up and anchored among the branches of three birch trees. Wood slats had been hammered onto one tree trunk, making it easy for the kids to climb up to the tree house. A wooden slide was attached to the back side of the play area, which looked as if it measured about ten feet square. Wood railings surrounded the rest of the play space so kids wouldn't fall off, and a slanted metal roof painted bright red made it a cozy hideout for rainy days.

"I had just got back from buying groceries early Tuesday morning when I heard gunshots," said DeeDee, standing under the tree house. "The kids were getting ready for school, so I assumed the sound that morning was unusually loud from the shooting range, so I didn't think too much about it. But as I was unloading my groceries in the kitchen, I looked out the kitchen window and saw that Danny up in our tree house. Right there." She pointed up as she was talking. "I ran outside, 'cause it dawned on me the two gunshots I'd heard sounded awful close, and sure enough, that kid was up there just randomly shooting away."

"Randomly?"

"Well, two shots, I guess. But that's enough to hurt someone, right? And if that happens, we get sued, right?" DeeDee looked at Lew with anxious eyes. "You can take that gun away from him, can't you?"

"I certainly can, and I will in a minute." Lew walked closer to the trees. She tested the makeshift ladder to see if it would support her 152 pounds.

"My husband climbs it," said DeeDee. "Don't worry, you can go up."

Up on the platform, Lew looked north and west out over the yard and past nearby treetops, her eyes searching until she saw it. Hoping she was right, she held her breath, but as she looked over the neighbor's rooftop and through the top branches of two young balsams, there was no mistaking it. She had a clear view of the small bay with the public beach, and across the little bay she could see the curve of the dirt road running along the front of the boys' camp and the tennis courts. They couldn't be much more than half a mile away.

No question, a rifle bullet shot by the neighbor kid from this tree house would have a good chance of hitting someone on that tennis court.

Scrambling down the ladder, she reached for her cell phone. After asking dispatch to put her through to youth services as an emergency, she identified herself and instructed the woman who had answered to send someone to meet her at DeeDee's house. "ASAP—this can't wait. I have a youngster running around with a loaded rifle."

"Someone will be right there," said the woman on the phone. "We know the family, and I've been waiting for a call like this. The father is out on probation, and we have been worried he has guns in the house. I'll have a deputy go along with my colleague. Thanks, Sheriff."

"I'll meet them there," said Lew. "I have questions for the boy."

Then she called Osborne. "Doc? Are you home or up at the tennis courts with Bruce?"

"I'm home for a short time," said Osborne. "What's up?"

"I need you to meet me—right away—here at DeeDee Burns' home on Pelican Place." She gave him the address, then said, "I need a second opinion. I may have found who shot Bert Willoughby—by accident."

"I'm on my way," said Osborne.

He arrived within minutes, and Lew and DeeDee walked him back to the tree house. Osborne climbed the ladder to stand on the platform and look north and northwest past the treetops. "I agree, Lewellyn," he said after checking out the angles. "You may have the answer."

"Good," said Lew, her relief tinged with sadness. "Now, if you and DeeDee will excuse me, I have to meet with youth services at this young man's house. And, yes, DeeDee, I'll be back to let you know how this goes. We'll get the guns out of that house, don't worry."

Leaving her cruiser in DeeDee's driveway, Lew ran down to the corner house, where she could see two cars. Someone from youth services and the deputy had already arrived.

In less than ten minutes, the deputy had arrested the boy's father for violating the terms of his probation by having firearms on the premises, and his son was turned over to the care of the social worker from youth services. As the social worker laid an arm across the frightened boy's shoulders to guide him to her car, Lew stepped forward. "Excuse me, I'm Sheriff Lew Ferris, and we need to talk before you leave with young Danny."

The woman nodded and waited until the boy entered the car before turning to Lew and replying. "Yes, Sheriff, I'm Lillian Herman, and thank you for your call. I'll be taking Danny to our juvenile counseling center—"

"That's what I need to talk to you about. Danny is a child, who may have fired a bullet that killed a man," said Lew as she glanced over at the boy in the back seat of the car. "But if so, it was an accident. The last thing I want—or that should happen—is for this young person to be traumatized by something he never intended to have happen, with a gun he never should have had access to. The question I have for you and for youth services is, how do we prevent that?"

Lillian looked at her in surprise. "I didn't know about the shooting. All I know is I was told to hurry out here and take charge of him because his father was going to be arrested and there is no mother. His mother died two years ago. So I'm assuming he will be put in foster care if no other relatives can be located quickly."

"That is exactly what worries me right now," said Lew. "This boy doesn't realize—he doesn't know yet—what happened. I worry what that news will do to him. So I don't want to see him put in a situation where he might not immediately get help in coping with all this. He needs help, Lillian. Professional help. And he needs it right now. Do you hear me?"

The social worker reached into her purse for her phone. "Bear with me, Sheriff Ferris," she said, "while I see if I can make a different arrangement. I know what you're saying, and it worries me too. Please tell me exactly what happened, then I will share the information with our director."

Lew explained the boy's behavior with the rifle and described how his random shooting from the tree house might well have caused the death of a well-known local dentist. When she finished, Lillian nodded and placed her call.

Lew listened as Lillian told her director how Danny had found his father's gun lying loose in the house, taken it outdoors to show it to the neighborhood kids, and fired it numerous times. Then she heard the social worker say, "One episode may have led to the death of a person quite a distance from where the boy was firing the gun. He doesn't know this yet, but Sheriff Ferris is very worried about the effect that will have on the child, on top of being removed from his home. We need to get him into special care." Lillian waited for an answer, then said, "I agree. I'll let Sheriff Ferris know. Thank you."

Lillian met Lew's eyes as she said, "This youngster isn't the first child we've had who found a gun left by a careless adult and used it in a way that injured or killed someone. My director just agreed with me that we'll send Danny to a childhood trauma center we work with in Green Bay. He'll be driven there later this afternoon and put in the care of the therapists there, who have experience with situations similar to this one."

"I'll want to know who will be working with this boy and how he's doing," said Lew, her tone resolute.

"Of course. I do too. Sheriff Ferris, if it's all right with you, I'll call you this evening and let you know that he's arrived at the trauma center, who will be working with him, and how he's doing."

"Good," said Lew. "Now, let me give you my personal cell number so you can reach me easily. And thank you, Lillian. It's heartbreaking to see how thoughtless the boy's father was, and the fact that he has no mother to take care of him now." Lew's voice wavered. "I don't know this boy, but I do know I want him to understand that what happened, which he will hear about, was not his fault. This was an accident. It doesn't have to ruin another life."

Lillian stepped forward to give Lew a brief hug. "I know, Sheriff Ferris. I have children too. I know this can be worse if we don't handle it with care and compassion for this boy and his life."

When the social worker had driven off with the young boy, Lew pulled on a pair of nitrile gloves and took possession of the rifle the boy had used as well as all unspent cartridges. She asked the deputy to be sure that the two handguns and any other weapons, such as hunting knives, were removed from the house.

With the rifle and a box of cartridges in hand, Lew walked back down to DeeDee's driveway, where DeeDee was waiting.

"Please, you don't have to worry, DeeDee," said Lew as she set the rifle and cartridges in the cruiser. "We have removed all the guns, and the boy, Danny, is being cared for by a kind woman with youth services, who is seeing that he will be taken to the childhood trauma center. They're prepared to help in situations like this, where a tragedy occurs. She'll keep me posted on how he does, and I'll share with you what I can."

"You're sure about all this?" DeeDee looked doubtful. "What about the father who let him have that gun?"

"He goes back to prison. Just owning the gun, much less having it in the house, is a serious violation of his parole. Also, I noticed that the house is up for sale, so when he does get out, he isn't likely to be back in this neighborhood."

"Thank you, Mrs. Ferris—I mean Sheriff. I can't thank you enough."

"DeeDee, I want you to feel confident you won't be dealing with this issue again. And if anything does worry you, you have my personal cell number. Just call." Lew walked over and gave DeeDee a warm hug. "Feeling better?"

At the expression of relief on the young woman's face, Lew hugged her once more before driving off.

A mile and a half down Loon Lake Road, she arrived at the dirt road facing the boys' camp. Up near the tennis courts, she could see the figures of Bruce and his investigators up near the tennis courts. Jumping out of her cruiser, Lew ran up to where Bruce was standing in conversation with one of the men.

"Sorry to interrupt," said Lew, "but you two have to follow me back down to where I'm parked on the road. I have something to show you, something you may find hard to believe."

The three of them walked down to the road and crossed it to stand at the top of the hill that sloped down toward the shoreline. "Look across that small bay," said Lew, pointing. "See the public beach and the houses over there?"

"Yeah," said Bruce and his colleague simultaneously.

"Well, if you had binoculars in your hand at this moment, you could see past a couple rooftops to a children's tree house . . ."

"Yeah," the men repeated, clearly wondering what was coming next.

"I just got hold of a rifle that a young kid used to stand in that tree house and shoot in this direction. Kid can't be more than ten, eleven years old, and the rifle belongs to his old man, who had no business having it in the house. More about that later, but I'm willing to bet money that the rifle I have sitting in my cruiser will answer the question of who shot Bert Willoughby."

To say Bruce looked surprised was an understatement. His colleague, too, was stunned. After studying the path across the bay and dropping his head in thought, Bruce said quietly, "Lew, I'll bet you're right. The distance, the sight line—it makes sense."

With that, Lew walked back to her cruiser, pulled on nitrile gloves, and reached for the rifle and cartridges. "Where would you like these?" she asked Bruce. "I'll give you directions so you can arrange to get a bullet that was shot into the tree by DeeDee Burns' house by the same rifle." She added, "DeeDee, by the way, is a close friend of my daughter's, which is how she knew to call me right away when the boy started using the rifle around her kids. I told her that you or one of your investigators may want to take a look at the tree house. I suggest you do."

"Good idea, and we'll get photos as well," said Bruce. "I'll get the rifle down to the lab right away. Our ballistics people should have an answer on this gun and the bullet that killed Dr. Willoughby by tomorrow morning, Lew."

Chapter Twenty

Katherine woke to the sound of her mother tromping up and down the stairs outside her bedroom door. When she couldn't stand it anymore, she poked her head out the door and hollered down the stairway. "Mom, you keep this up and I'm heading back to my place. What on earth are you doing?"

"Trying to clean up for the funeral, and I can't find my good duster—"

"What funeral? What are you talking about?"

"The Wausau Crime Lab called half an hour ago. They now know for sure Bert was shot by accident, so I can have the funeral home get ready, and I just called our minister, and he's scheduling Bert's funeral for Tuesday morning. This house is going to be crawling with people, and I want everything perfect."

Katherine sighed. "Deb will do it. Why don't you settle down, Mom? That's what you pay her for."

"Not the landing, and all my precious Ming vases. I don't let her touch those, and now I can't find my duster. You know, the one with the long handle."

"Oh god," said Katherine, closing the bedroom door. Then she had a thought. She knew she had to do something before it became known that there was a clause in the will stating that in the event of Robin Carpenter's remarriage or death, the trust would revert to the Willoughby family to be inherited by Jane and Katherine. If that got out, she was sure would become a prime suspect. How to dodge that? She knew she could think of something. She always had been able to.

With the sounds of her mother bustling about downstairs, Katherine hurried to get dressed. She wanted to be the morning's first visitor to the office of the sheriff of McBride County, and she wanted to look professional.

* * *

Deb was busy giving the kitchen floor a quick mopping when Jane burst in behind her, her voice high and shrill. "Dammit, Deb, where did you hide my duster? I've looked everywhere."

"In the garage, where it always is," said Deb, pausing over her mop. "Hold on, I'll check for it." Out in the garage, she found the long-handled duster hanging in its usual spot, though a rake had slipped sideways, covering the lower half. She grabbed the duster and went back into the kitchen.

Looking down at it, she said to Jane, "This is pretty worn. I'll be at the hardware store later this morning. Would you like me to get a new head for it? They aren't expensive, and a new one would be less likely to scratch those vases of yours."

"Good idea—the sooner the better," said Jane, who, Deb noticed for the umpteenth time, rarely said thank-you.

After removing the worn head from the duster, Deb took the handle back to the garage. On the way, she picked up a sack of discarded newspapers to throw in the recycle bin. Opening the bin, she threw in the sack of papers. As she was closing the lid, her eye caught the edge of something colorful in one corner.

She lifted the lid again and pushed empty shoeboxes out of the way. A jacket? No, a hooded sweatshirt. *Worn, but what a great color.* Deb pulled it out of the bin and gave it a quick try-on. Fit surprisingly well. She rolled it up and set it next to her purse on the table by the door that opened to the kitchen. What a good find! Her fleece jacket was just about worn out, and the hoodie would be perfect for her early-morning walk.

Deb counted on those early-morning walks to keep her sane. The constant bending and lifting of housework could leave her too tired to exercise late in the day, so she walked at five in the morning. The daily walks plus a strenuous workout on Sundays at Anytime Fitness kept her feeling lithe and energetic. As long as she kept her spirits up, she didn't mind working for crabby, mean old Jane. The money was good, and that was what mattered.

* * *

Lew sat thinking as Judith and Dani waited patiently. All three had notepads in front of them. All three notepads were empty.

"Well," said Lew after a long pause, "maybe I start with one of Robin Carpenter's girlfriends. They might know something."

"I'll call the salon and see if anyone there knows someone too," said Dani, trying to sound helpful.

"Was she ever married?" asked Judith. "Any angry exhusbands lurking out there?"

"Good thought," said Lew, jotting a note. "I can torture myself and call Pecore. He'll know if she's been married or not."

"He may know her close friends too," said Dani. "But why not have one of your deputies make these calls, Sheriff? You've got enough going on."

"At the risk of sounding obnoxious, I think I may be better at this, given the victim is female. I feel like I read body language better than some men may. Could be wrong, but I want to stay on top of this myself."

"I think you're right," said Judith. "Could be that a small detail points you in the right direction. What about that pickleball player who was injured when Robin Carpenter and Dr. Willoughby played him and his partner?"

"Not likely, but I better check it out," said Lew. She didn't want to say that her "not likely" was based on intuition, not fact. And that was why she knew she'd better check it out. *Intuition* was not a chapter in the law enforcement manuals.

"This is a non sequitur and certainly not helpful, but I've been meaning to mention it sometime," said Dani.

"What's that?" asked Lew. "Never know until you say it."

"I just want to point out that both those Willoughby women used to come to our salon, and would you believe they never tipped, despite being well off? I mean, every single one of our other clients tips at least twenty percent. Now, I only work Saturdays at the salon, but we all knew about those two—Jane and Katherine. Everyone got so tired of their meanness and overall negativity. The two stylists who had been working with them finally had it. One day they worked up the courage to flat out tell Jane and Katherine that if they wanted their hair done, they would have to go somewhere else." That said, Dani sat back with a satisfied look on her face.

"Well, the old man was cheap, so must be family tradition," said Lew, grinning. "Again, Dani, that info may come in handy. You never know. Okay, you two, one last item we need to cover today—"

"Press conference," said Judith. "Before you say another word, Lew, we are getting *bombarded* by the press."

"I know, I know, and that's exactly where I was going. Assuming I have no luck arresting anyone today—and even if I do—let's plan a press conference for three thirty this afternoon. I can at least give the public an update, and that gives both the paper and the television reporters time to meet their deadlines."

"It's a plan indeed," said Judith, getting to her feet. "I think, too, that if you have no person of interest for Robin's death by three, then we should make one of Diane's photos available. See if someone watching the news recognizes the figure."

"Good idea, but that's a long shot," said Lew. "If only . . ." She raised her eyebrows, looking hopeful.

"Hey," said Dani as she headed for the door, "who knows where my tipping story might take you too. Worth a try, Sheriff."

* * *

Lew had just poured herself a cup of coffee and was about to call Pecore when dispatch called to say she had a visitor. "This early?" Lew checked the time. It was eight fifteen.

"Dr. Katherine Willoughby," said Arlene on dispatch. "Send her down?"

A minute later, after a knock on the door, the tall, broad-shouldered woman walked into Lew's office. "Sorry to interrupt your morning, Sheriff, but I need to share important information before you hear it from the wrong people."

"Sit down, please," said Lew, pointing to one of the chairs in front of her desk as she hit a button on her phone. Raising a hand before Katherine could say anything, Lew said, "Judith, I need you in my office again. Sorry."

As Judith hurried into the room, Lew introduced her. "My senior administrator, Judith Hanson. Judith, please take the chair next to Dr. Willoughby." Lew looked at Katherine and said, "We have a great deal going on right now, so I want both of us to hear what you have to say. Do you mind, Dr. Willoughby?"

"Not in the least," said Katherine, her head high and her voice resolute, as if she was prepared to rebut anyone who didn't like what she was about to say. "What I have to tell you will be public knowledge after probate anyway. It's about my father's will, and—"

"Sorry to interrupt, but your mother did let you know that we've confirmed his death was an accident?" Lew asked.

"Yes, and that is a relief to know, except . . ." She dropped her head as if holding back tears. "What you don't know is something so difficult for me to talk about, but . . . my mom and dad . . . well, they weren't getting along. They've always bickered, you know, but I had no idea Dad was . . . filing for divorce."

"Oh, that has to be difficult for you, I'm sure," said Lew. Judith nodded in sympathy too.

"And he was very romantically involved with that woman."

"What woman? The one who was killed?" Lew asked.

"Yes, but that's not all." Katherine took a deep breath. "He left her a lot of money in his will. A lot. My mom was stunned."

Judith sat forward in her chair. "Are you saying your father cut your mother out of the will?"

"No, oh, gosh, no, he left Mom and me plenty of money. Just that his lawyer is sure to tell you that with Dad leaving thousands of dollars to that woman . . . well . . ."

"I see," said Lew. "Do you have any reason to think that your mom . . . ?"

"No, absolutely not. She hasn't touched a rifle since she and Dad stopped hunting together years ago. No, I'm sure not."

"Where was your mother yesterday morning around six AM?

"Home, I'm sure. I was asleep, but I'm sure she was home. But I thought it very important that you hear this from me. Mom is devastated by Dad's death, and she sure as heck doesn't need anyone to suspect that she would have anything to do with it."

"Of course," said Lew. "I think it's quite good you told us."

"Do you have any idea who might have shot Miss Carpenter?" asked Judith, looking up from her notepad, where she'd been busy writing.

"Gosh, not really. I never met the woman, so I wouldn't know."

"Who is the lawyer you mentioned?" asked Lew.

"Robert Portman. Bob is what Dad called him."

"Sure. I know Bob Portman," said Lew, deciding not to add that Bob Portman tied very nice trout flies. "Anything more you want us to know?"

Katherine raised her eyebrows and wiped at her eyes. "I just hope no one has to bother my mom with all this, y'know. Her life is hard enough right now."

After Lew and Judith had walked Katherine to the door, the two women headed back to Lew's desk, sat down, and stared at each other for a long moment.

"What do *you* think?" Lew asked at last.

"At the risk of sounding mean-spirited, I think she just threw her mother under the bus."

Lew nodded. "I think I need to make a phone call," she said. "Bob Portman."

"Keep me updated," said Judith. "I'm off to call a couple reporters."

Lew picked up the phone and called Portman's office.

"Mr. Portman is out of the office this weekend," his secretary told her. "He's on a fishing trip to the UP—the Two-Hearted River. He's due back on Monday."

Disappointed, Lew made the call she'd been dreading: to the McBride County coroner, Ed Pecore. Unfortunately, he *was* in the office.

Chapter Twenty-One

On her way to the dental office, Katherine gave her steering wheel a happy slap.

"Good job, girl. You told 'em just enough to keep them happy," she said to herself. "They don't need to know any more, and they won't until months from now when Dad's will finally goes to probate." She made a mental note to encourage her mother to challenge something minor in the will, as that would delay probate even longer. The longer the better.

"And when it's read," she continued to remind herself, "you just lie and tell everyone you had no idea Dad was determined to give that woman so much money. You can say your mom knew, but you were never told. After all, Bob Portman was the executor, not you, not Jane."

Yes, Katherine was satisfied. Even the fact that the Willoughby dental practice was about to be sold no longer bothered her. Why should it? It was now guaranteed that she would be wealthy. She would never have to work another day. And that was fine with her. She never had liked being a dentist; she'd only done it to get attention from her dad.

"Life is good, girl," she said out loud as she pulled into her parking space at the office. She was a little taken aback to see that Robin Steadman was there, but that was hardly a problem. All she planned to do that morning was rescue the cash she'd discovered in Bert's desk drawer. That needed to put in a secure place—aka her purse. She grinned to herself.

"Hello-o-o," she called as she walked into the darkened waiting room. "Robin? You here?"

"Back in the lab," came the sound of Robin Steadman's voice. "Getting things ready for the crown work you need to do next week."

"Crown work? What crown work?" asked Katherine as she walked toward Bert's office.

"I thought I mentioned to you that I have two of your dad's patients who need their crown work completed. Bert had it underway, so completing those shouldn't be difficult. Oh, and your mom called a little while ago and told me the funeral will be held Tuesday, so I've arranged for the patients to come in Monday morning. You don't have any appointments early that day. Is that okay? I can always change their appointments."

"No, that should work fine."

Robin Steadman poked her head out into the hall as Katherine was walking by and said, "I've asked the cleaning crew to hold off today and clean over the weekend instead. You know they usually come on Friday afternoons, but I wanted to try to have your dad's chair and instruments all put away. Do you think you'll want to use that room for any of your patients before the new owners take over?"

"No, thank you, though," said Katherine. Once she was in Bert's office, she closed the door, reached for the key, which she had slipped into a side pocket in her purse, and unlocked the desk drawer. Just as she was reaching into the drawer for the cash, Robin knocked and opened the door. Before she could see anything, Katherine managed to slide the desk drawer closed.

"I was wondering if there is anything here that your mother might like to have," said Robin. "Any of your father's framed photos or the framed documents from when he was awarded his DDS?"

"You know, I better ask her," said Katherine, deciding to get the cash another time rather than risk Robin seeing it and seeing her take it. She doubted Robin had any idea that Bert had kept that much cash in his drawer—or his reason for doing so. God forbid Katherine have to answer questions about her dad and how it was he kept so much money in the office. She wasn't sure herself what he'd been up to. "Let's leave everything where it is for the time being, and I'll be back when I know what she would like. Very thoughtful of you, Robin. Thank you."

Back in her car, she heaved a sigh of relief. The day, so far, had gone well.

* * *

Deep in thought at her desk, Lew waited for Pecore to arrive. She was mulling over Katherine's visit. The woman had certainly gone out of her way to prepare Lew for the gossip sure to surface about Bert Willoughby and his personal life. Maybe it helped her feel less ashamed of her father's behavior.

Yes, he'd fooled around, and, yes, Robin Carpenter had been his current playmate. Yes, he'd been planning to divorce Jane. And, yes, he'd left his girlfriend some big bucks.

A knock sounded on Lew's door, and she braced herself, but the person who stuck their head in was Dani Wright and not the frequently hungover coroner.

"Sheriff, can we talk before you meet with Mr. Pecore? He's the dead woman's uncle, right?"

"The *victim's* uncle," said Lew with a gentle correction. "Yes, come in. What do you have?"

"Like you asked, I did a couple searches on Robin Carpenter—ran one on Google and the other through our law enforcement databases. And, boy, did I hit pay dirt."

"Really," said Lew, brightening up.

"Yes. She has an arrest record in Chicago, though she was never incarcerated."

"Really?" Lew sat up straighter. "That sounds strange."

"Turns out she and a couple girlfriends got into the modeling biz." Dani waved the pen she was holding in the air. "*Kind of* the modeling biz, may I say. They got hired by some operation to perform short X-rated performances that were uploaded to a website. People could access the videos for a price. The girls got a percentage.

"When the people running the website got arrested, apparently for stealing customers' data or something like that, the girls were arrested, too, for being involved in the data theft. But Robin Carpenter agreed to be an informant, so no charges were pressed. She was free to go.

"That was over a year ago, Sheriff. I also checked into that kind of operation—"

"X-rated modeling?"

"Yep. Those gals make a lot of money. I would bet you Robin Carpenter has a few bucks in the bank. One of the documents I saw online said the women made over a hundred grand doing their thing. I can see why. If you look at photos of Robin Carpenter from then, she was a humdinger. I can see why that old man liked her." Dani held up a screen-shot she had printed off. "Nice looking, doncha think?"

Lew studied the photo, then agreed. "Very pretty and well-to-do by Loon Lake standards. Assuming he didn't know where she got her money, a woman like that would certainly appeal to a man like Willoughby. And I imagine our victim was not against currying the favor of an older, wealthy man. Question I have is, how on earth did she get into pickleball?"

An alert from dispatch on her phone told Lew that Pecore had arrived.

"Thanks, Dani. Pecore's here, and this info is very helpful. I'll check back with you after I talk to him."

Dani paused at the door to say, "I would wonder one thing, Sheriff. If the dead woman informed on those data thieves, would one of them come looking for her?"

"Good point," said Lew. "Since she was arrested but never charged, she had to have shared important information. I wonder if Uncle Ed knows about all this?"

"Good luck," said Dani, raising her eyebrows and giving Lew a wide grin.

*   *   *

A pudgy man with a jowly face and gray hair combed wetly over his balding skull strode head down into Lew's office. He yanked at one of the chairs in front of her desk so hard it seemed he expected it to run away.

"Take a seat, Ed," said Lew after the fact. She had to hide an inappropriate smile. "Sorry for the news on your niece."

"Same creep shot Dr. Willoughby got her," said Ed. "I warned you about that, but you didn't believe me. You got a murderer out there, dammit, Ferris."

"I know you'd feel better if that was true, Ed, but I got a report in late yesterday that the Wausau boys confirmed the bullet that hit Dr. Willoughby was fired by a young boy randomly shooting his dad's gun to show off. He was over on Pelican Drive and up on a kids' tree house, which gave him a straight shot over the bay by the public beach. Bert's death was a complete accident."

"You have no business letting kids have guns," said Pecore, sputtering.

"Couldn't agree with you more," said Lew, nodding. "Do you mind if I ask you a few questions about your niece? Because you're right—she was murdered." She did her best to give a man she detested a sympathetic look. "Your Robin was a lovely young woman. I can tell she was quite attractive."

Ed sat up a little straighter as he said, "Yep, my sister raised her right. Pretty and a very successful fashion model. 'Extreme fashion' is what she told me she did. She promised to show me sometime."

Lew let that one go. "Do you think she had any, you know, people who resented her success or might have been out to get her? Just looking for a lead here, Ed . . ."

"God no, that girl was perfect."

Lew nodded. Clearly the man had no clue. "Maybe I should talk to her mother?"

"Nah. Marie died three years ago." He thought for a moment. "Maybe her best friend, Chrissy? She might know something. Those two been close since grade school."

"Do you have a number where I can reach her?"

"No, but she bartends at the Antler Inn most nights."

"Good, I'll stop by and tell her you told me she could help."

"Ferris?"

"What, Ed?"

"You sure it was the kid's gun killed the dentist? I could swear that looked intentional to me."

"Ballistics matched the bullet to the rifle, Ed. And no exit wound speaks to the bullet hitting with less impact and coming from far away. No question in my mind. You are certainly free to call down to the Wausau Crime Lab if you wish."

Pecore shrugged and got up to leave.

Watching him walk out of her office, Lew marveled, as she always did, that he'd gotten appointed county coroner simply because he was the brother-in-law of the Loon Lake mayor. Of course, the mayor was a man influential in local politics. Influential enough that he could appoint an official whose credentials for determining an individual's cause of death—aside from the family connection—were limited to having worked as a bartender and getting pretty over-served himself.

Chapter
Twenty-Two

∼

After scarfing down a quick lunch at her desk, Lew headed out to the Antler Inn. She found the woman she assumed to be Chrissy Tolbert on her knees, cleaning behind the bar. "Hey, be with you in a minute. Just trying to wipe stuff up," said the woman, without glancing up to see who owned the footsteps she'd heard.

After a few minutes, she got to her feet. "Yes, can I help you? We don't open for another thirty minutes, so you'll have to have to have something nonalcoholic until then." She studied Lew's uniform and badge with a concerned expression on her face. "We're strict here," she added. "What'll it be?"

"Nothing, thank you," said Lew, sliding onto a barstool. "Do you happen to know where I can find Chrissy Tolbert?"

"That's me," said the woman, tossing the dishrag in her hand into a nearby sink and pushing strands of dark hair back behind her ears. "Is this about Robin Carpenter? Her uncle told me you might be by."

"Yes, I'm Sheriff Lew Ferris. Ed Pecore and I work together. He told me you and Robin were close friends. Do you mind if I ask you a few questions? I want to find the person who killed her."

"That makes two of us," said the woman, looking teary-eyed. She wiped at her face. "Sorry. Hard to lose your best friend, y'know." After pouring herself a glass of water, Chrissy walked around the bar and came over to sit on one of the barstools near Lew. She set a cell phone down on the counter, reached back to pull an elastic band off her pony-tail, shook her head, and redid the ponytail. Then she gave Lew a long look that turned into a soft sob as she dropped her face into her hands.

Lew sat silent, waiting. Chrissy had to be in her early thirties, the same age as Robin Carpenter. She was about five feet six, slim but not skinny, with pale skin and straight dark-brown hair. She seemed to have some makeup on but not a lot, maybe a little lipstick. She was wearing dark jeans and a light-green long-sleeved shirt with large cream-colored letters that read THE ANTLER INN.

Lew sensed the woman put in long days and likely had several kids at home. After a minute or two, Chrissy reached for a napkin in a wooden box sitting on the bar, wiped at her face, and gave Lew a weak smile. "I apologize, but knowing I was going to talk about my Robbie just kinda hit me, y'know?"

"I do. Take your time. I'm in no rush."

"Well, Robbie and I lived next door to each other grow-ing up, and we were pretty close until she married Fred

Murphy and they moved to Evanston. He worked for one of the big hospitals there as a manager of cleaning services. Robbie had a job in the hospital's day care center. But about eight years after they married, she left him. That's when she got in trouble."

Chrissy gave Lew a skeptical look as she said, "If I tell you about that, are you going to tell her uncle Ed?"

"Nope, not a word," said Lew, before Chrissy could say more. "All that is none of Ed's business, but I need to know."

"I think you should, because she got in with some pretty creepy no-goodniks, if you know what I mean. And I really think if my good friend had used her head, this might not have happened—"

Chrissy jumped off her stool and ran back behind the bar to grab her purse. "Look at this, will you?" She held out a small photo of her friend as she said, "Robbie was gorgeous, see? No reason for her to have fooled around with a bunch of coke crazies, y'know?"

Lew glanced at the photo. Chrissy was right—Robin Carpenter had been a pretty, lively-eyed girl. "Any idea what made her do it?"

"Sure. I asked her, 'cause I couldn't believe she would be so stupid. And she said it was the money. You gotta remember, Robbie and me—we grew up in families that didn't have a lot of money. So when a couple girls she knew from her work at the hospital said they were making a couple thousand a month, Robbie checked it out."

Chrissy paused for a moment before continuing. "She got hired right away. She said it was the easiest money she ever made. She told me all she had to do was take her clothes off and dance around a little. And someone paid big bucks to watch. That was all—at least that's what she told me. Now, if that's the whole story, I don't know. I wouldn't be surprised if it wasn't, y'know. Robbie was my friend, but she wasn't perfect."

"Did she know the people she was working for were stealing their customers' data? Data that allowed them to use credit cards and empty bank accounts?"

Chrissy shook her head. "You know, Robbie didn't tell me much. What she did say was that when they got caught and she was arrested, all she did was give the cops the names of the people she worked for. They were happy with that, and that's why they let her go."

"They let her go under certain conditions," said Lew. "Chrissy, this is helpful information, so thank you." She could tell from the expression on Chrissy's face that the woman didn't know much more, but it was worth asking. "Do you happen to know if she was ever contacted by some of those people—the ones who had been arrested after she named them? Anyone threaten her?"

Chrissy stared down at the countertop, thinking, before replying slowly, "Yeah, maybe . . . right after she moved up here. She only mentioned it once or twice, and then all of sudden she was dating that old man and that's all she would talk about. That rich dentist. She was all about that guy all the time, y'know?"

"Sure, that's natural," said Lew, her voice kind. "But going back to any threats. Did she mention any names?"

"The only one she really talked about was the guy that her boyfriend, the dentist, hurt. You know about that, right?"

Lew raised her eyebrows. "No, not sure what you're talking about."

"Well, here's what happened—but first you need to know something Robbie does that kind of made it her fault." Chrissy paused, and Lew waited. "Robbie has always done this one thing around men. She did it with boys when we were in high school, and she still did it." Chrissy lowered her voice as if she was afraid people were listening. "Robbie was all about getting attention from men. She wore lots of makeup always, she kept her hair perfect, and she had this way of looking up at guys as if she was in love with them. Do you know what I mean?"

"Flirting?"

"More than that. More bedroomy, if you know what I mean . . ."

"Seductive?"

"Seductive. Yes! Good word, Sheriff. She was always *seductive* with men. That's how she got that older dentist to fall in love with her. See, Robbie was good at softball when we were girls, so when she moved back here, she decided to play pickleball. She wanted me to play too. 'C'mon, Chrissy,' she'd say, 'it is so easy to play and a great way to meet guys.'"

"Probably true," said Lew, nodding.

"So first she met the dentist, and they were playing together. I guess they were a team, and when they played this other couple, Robbie thought that guy was cute too, so

At the Edge of the Woods

she was being kind of . . . seductive with him. When the dentist saw that, he got jealous, hauled off and smashed a ball right into the guy's groin. Guy had to go to the hospital it was so bad."

"When did this happen?" asked Lew.

"Maybe two weeks ago. Anyway, that guy got so mad he kept calling the dentist and Robbie and telling them he was going to sue."

"And you know this man's name?"

"I do, because he thought she worked here, so he called here a couple times. Tim is his name. Tim Beskind. He and his partner were the top pickleball players in the region before he was injured. He was so angry he swore he'd show old Bert just how it felt." Chrissy paused. "Robbie didn't worry at first, but then it got weird. She saw the guy following her around the pickleball courts when they were competing in Wausau a couple weeks ago. She said he stayed back like he was hiding, but she saw him. She said it gave her the creeps."

Lew filed away this information in her head and switched back to the earlier topic. "Going back for a minute to the people she made the videos for in Chicago, did you say someone did call Robin? Or drive up here and threaten her?"

"I think so, but that was a while ago when she first got here. I don't remember her saying any names. I'm sorry, I don't."

"That's okay. I can check with law enforcement on the case. I may get back to you to run some names by you and see if any sound familiar. Or if you do think of any after I leave, here's my cell number. Just give me a call, please."

Lew handed Chrissy her card. She was about to leave when Chrissy started talking again.

"That dentist. He's pretty rich, right?"

"Not sure, Chrissy. I've known people in health care like dentists and doctors to do pretty well financially, so I imagine he had money. Why?"

Chrissy brightened as she said, "Robbie told me she was going to marry the guy and be rich, rich, rich. She said he swore he would take all his money and spend it on her. Just her, but . . ." She hadn't finished her sentence before her expression grew somber. "Guess that didn't happen, did it."

"No, it did not," said Lew, shaking her head. "Chrissy, thank you for your time, and please call me if you think of anything else that might help my investigation. I am so sorry for what happened to your friend." Lew reached over to give the woman's arm a sympathetic squeeze.

"Good reason not to do 'seductive,' doncha think?" said Chrissy, attempting a smile as she walked with Lew to the entrance to the bar.

As Lew headed toward her cruiser, she thought about the word *seductive*. That was one behavior she had never been good at.

Chapter
Twenty-Three

~

After asking Dani to find a phone number and address for Tim Beskind, Lew checked in with Judith, who had left a voice mail saying she needed to reach her ASAP. Feeling frustrated with her lack of progress on who might have killed Robin Carpenter, Lew crossed her fingers. Maybe Judith was calling with a good lead—a break in the case, maybe. But in her gut she knew better.

"What's up? Not another—"

"No, no," said Judith, "but I thought you'd like to know that the pickleball players have canceled their upcoming tournament. They keep calling here to see if we've arrested the person who shot Robin Carpenter. They're very worried that it may be some nut out to get more of the players."

"I can understand that," said Lew. "Tell them we're following all leads and we'll be in touch as soon as we know more. I understand their concern."

"Unless you do find out anything, the press conference is set for three thirty this afternoon."

"Good. Right now my sense is we'll need that. I have to jump; Dani's calling with a number I asked her to get."

* * *

Tim Beskind lived in a contemporary rust-colored frame house nestled into a hill behind the Loon Lake High School. When Lew pulled into the spacious parking area below a balcony running along the front of the house, a tall, slim man stepped onto the balcony to look down at her. She guessed him to be in his late fifties.

"Can I help you, Officer?" he asked in a polite tone.

"I'm Sheriff Lew Ferris, and if you're Tim Beskind, I'd like to speak with you about the shooting at the Willoughby property yesterday."

"Certainly. I'll be right down."

Within minutes, he had welcomed her into a small family room on the lower level and introduced himself. "I was sorry to hear about Bert Willoughby," said Tim, "even though he and I were not the best of friends."

"I understand he could be aggressive on the ball court," said Lew, "but this is about his partner."

"Robin Carpenter? I think that's her name. Am I wrong?"

"No, that's her name. You know she was shot and killed yesterday on the same property, the old tennis courts, where Dr. Willoughby was accidentally shot?"

"What? No, I did not know that," said Tim. "How did *that* happen? I've been in Madison and just got back an hour ago. I hadn't heard—"

"That's what we're trying to find out," said Lew. "I'm talking with everyone who might have some information that could help us out. Someone mentioned you were planning to sue Dr. Willoughby and may have made some angry phone calls?"

"Yes, I did make the calls. I made them because I felt Bert Willoughby was taking it too far. He was going to seriously hurt someone if he kept up that behavior. I had decided not to sue, but only because I started feeling better." He looked at Lew more closely. "But what about that young woman? You're saying someone shot her?"

"Yes. Early yesterday morning. Were you in Madison then?"

"Yes, but please, I'm a retired highway engineer. I can assure you I don't go around shooting people. I don't even hit the pickleball hard, certainly not hard enough to cause the kind of bruising Bert Willoughby does. I mean did. Sorry, I shouldn't say things like that."

"What about other pickleball players? Are you aware of other people who may have been playing with Dr. Willoughby and Robin Carpenter?"

"You mean . . . who also got hit too hard? No, I don't."

Lew turned to walk out the door, saying, "I appreciate your time, Tim. And I'm glad you're feeling better."

A woman walked down the stairs just then and stopped to say, "Sheriff, another question you might want to ask is, who was that woman seeing besides Dr. Willoughby?"

"Excuse me, and you are—?" Lew gave her an inquisitive look.

"Tim's wife, Clare. Sorry to intrude, but when I heard you say there's been another shooting, I thought you should know that woman was known to hang around the bars, and who knows what she was up to. I heard some rumors . . . No!" She waved at her husband. "Dammit, Tim, don't tell me to shut up. Robin Carpenter told a couple women I know that she had once had a very popular website or app or something like that that she made a ton of money on. She had to give it up or go to jail because someone else in her group was stealing from people. From what I heard, she was pretty proud of these skanky videos of hers." The woman's face twisted in disdain.

"I don't think that has anything to do with what Sheriff Ferris is investigating," said Tim, dismissing his wife's story with a shake of his head.

"Actually, it has everything to do with it," Lew said, and nodded at Clare, encouraging her to say more. "Did anyone you know ever actually see one of the videos?"

"No, we only ever heard about them. I mean, who would want to?" Her voice was filled with indignation.

"I ask because it could have been someone connected to that operation who could tell us more about what's happened."

"That's as much as I know," said Clare. "I play pickleball too, and I was there that day when Bert slammed his ball into Tim. He did it not to win but because that girlfriend of his was all over my husband."

Tim's eyes widened. He looked taken aback at his wife's reaction but didn't say anything.

After getting the names of the friends of Clare's who might have heard about Robin Carpenter's videos, Lew drove back to her office.

*   *   *

"I have no new leads," said Lew to the two women looking at her with expectant expressions on their faces. "Nothing. But Robin Carpenter had a chapter in her life that may hold the answer."

"Those sleazy videos, right?" asked Dani. "I followed up on that court case for you, but aside from Robin and two other women who were performing for the distributors, they're all still in prison and will be for a while."

"That's not to say they didn't ask someone else to go after Carpenter," said Judith. "Who knows if she had more information that law enforcement didn't know about yet?"

"*Yet.* Good point," said Lew. She exhaled in frustration. "The more I learn, the more it looks like that young woman was as squirrely as—"

Judith raised a hand. "Don't say it, Lewellyn." She laughed. "Whatever dumb things Ed Pecore does, at least he keeps his clothes on."

The three of them had a good laugh.

"Okay." Lew slapped her desk. "On to the press confer-ence. You never know who knows what."

"I'm ready with a good blowup of one of Diane's photos for the newspapers and an even better one for the television cameras. TV is our best bet. You can see the color—"

"And the movement," said Judith. "Dani did a nice job, so the series of shots make it look like the person is running even though they're still photos."

*   *   *

Lew had Bruce Peters open the press conference. She wanted the public to know that Dr. Bert Willoughby's death had been an accident—and to alert other parents to the dangers of children having easy access to guns. She had invited Diane Knutsen to attend, too, in case there were any questions on the photos.

Once Bruce had completed his report, Lew went over the details surrounding the shooting death of Robin Carpenter. She introduced the photos that she hoped might be familiar to someone reading the newspaper or viewing the television news. People were encouraged to call the McBride County Sheriff's Department with any information, even if they couldn't identify the image in the photo. If they had seen anything suspicious at all, they were asked to "please call."

"Good luck with that," said Bruce after the news reporters and television crews had left the room. "I took some time with those photos myself," he said, "but I cannot imagine anyone recognizing that figure. There just isn't enough to see, Lew."

"I agree," said Diane, who was standing nearby. "I wish I had been able to see more through all those branches and pine needles, darn it."

"I know," said Lew, sounding dejected. "But we have to start somewhere."

"What time is it?" asked Bruce as the last person left the conference room.

"Four o'clock," said Lew. "Time for me to catch up on my paperwork."

"Hell, no," said Bruce with lively eyebrows. "Time to see what's hatching on the Prairie. That's what time it is."

"He's one hundred percent correct," said a voice from the back of the room. Lew turned to see Osborne walking toward her. "I was coming to invite you to my place tonight," he said, "but I believe the Prairie is on the way."

Lew laughed. "Yeah, but I have an idea too. Let's include that young woman who took those photos."

"Really? I can come too?" asked Diane, looking so happy that everyone burst out laughing. "What do I need to bring?"

"Not a thing," said Lew. "Between me, Doc Osborne, and Bruce here, we've got you covered."

Chapter
Twenty-Four

Taking care not to break the speed limit, Lew raced out to her farm to drop off the cruiser, change into her khakis, and check to be sure she had enough gas in Nellie, her trusty pickup. It had been nearly a week since she'd been able to restore her soul on the trout stream. In less than ten minutes, she had her clothes changed, her fly rods in the back seat, Nellie ready for the gas station—and Lew was ready for the Prairie River.

As she drove, she noticed the evening might be signaling an early winter. There was a chill in the air as the sky, struggling to keep the sun up, surrounded it with streaks of fuchsia and dove gray. As she pulled into the clearing along the trout stream, the sight of pale-gold pools of light among the riffles lifted Lew's heart, and the soft burble of the flowing water reminded her that life was not all about work.

She spotted Diane Knutsen right away. The young woman was sitting on one of the large boulders near the bank of the Prairie, waiting patiently. Bruce had already waded into the Prairie and was heading upstream. At the sound of Nellie's arrival, he turned back to give a quick wave before disappearing around the first bend in the shallow stream. Osborne was leaning against the driver's seat of his Subaru as he pulled his waders on.

Lew, pointing toward where Bruce had disappeared, said, "Put that man near water, and he turns hyperactive."

"That's a good way to put it," said Diane with a laugh. "I've never seen anyone pull on a pair of waders so fast."

"Head on over here, Diane," said Lew, smiling as she dropped open the hatch at the back of her pickup. "I've got waders and a rod you can use today—"

"Excuse me, Lew," said Osborne, interrupting her as he walked toward them, waders on and fly rod in hand. "I'm going in to practice my double haul for the umpteenth time. Let me know if you need anything."

"We'll be fine," said Lew, "but, Doc, remember to keep your arm flexed at the end of that hauling move. You always try to straighten it out."

"I know, I know," said Osborne, shaking his head. "I'll get it right one of these days." He looked at Diane as he said, "By the way, Miss Knutsen, count your blessings. You're about to get a lesson from an expert, the best fly-fishing instructor short of the famous Joan Wulff."

"Hey, enough baloney, Doc," said Lew, waving at him to keep going. "Now, go get in the water and don't spook the trout." After Osborne had walked past them and started wading into the shallow streambed, Lew said, "He's embarrassing me, Diane. The woman he mentioned, Joan Wulff, is an icon in the fly-fishing world. I was lucky enough to take lessons from her. When my students find they like this sport, I encourage them to take the time and make the trip to enroll in her fly-fishing school in upstate New York."

"Sheriff Ferris, I'm feeling pretty darn lucky right now," said Diane as she pulled on the waders that Lew had handed her. "Here I am with you on the Prairie River, and then on Sunday Ray Pradt has offered to take me muskie fishing. Is this amazing or what?" She grinned.

"Have you fished muskie before?" asked Lew.

"Never. In fact, I really haven't fished much in my life. I grew up in Los Angeles and my parents were golfers, so I had very little exposure to fishing. Maybe they talked about it at my Scout camp, but I never tried it."

"Then you are about to discover there's a big difference between fly-fishing and fishing for muskie or walleye or other bait fish," said Lew, walking Diane down to the stream bank. "When you fly-fish, you're *in* the water. When you bait fish, you're *on* the water.

"I kid my fly-fishing students that they need to remember that when you're in the water, you're on public land, but once you step out, you're on private land. *And who knows who lives there*," Lew said, lowering her voice to a comic level. "Seriously, though, for me, spending time in the trout stream means finding solitude. I have used time in the trout stream to grieve, and I have used it to celebrate. At the risk of sounding goofy, my heart is in the trout stream. On the other hand, many people, like Ray, prefer bait fishing, which can be fishing from a boat, from a dock, from a pontoon. And that often means fishing with or close to other people. If you're like Doc, you may prefer one but enjoy both. He fished muskie for years and took up fly-fishing just three years ago. He still does both, but most often these days, he prefers fly-fishing."

"Hmm," said Diane. "What I know right now is that, oddly enough, having been in a place where I nearly witnessed a murder has turned out to be a strange gift. The experience—because it has led to meeting you and Bruce, Doc, and Ray—is handing me the opportunity to learn about the outdoors in a way I haven't before. I am so lucky."

"Well, let's see what you think after I show you how to hold a fly rod," said Lew with a chuckle as the two women walked into the trout stream.

When they reached a spot where there were few branches overhanging the stream, Lew paused to say, "Now, Diane, how you hold your fly rod is critical, so please watch." Gripping her fly rod, she extended her arm. "You want to keep your thumb on top of the grip like this . . ." Lew held her rod out so Diane could see what she meant. "Doing this correctly is the difference between a good, controlled cast or a mess."

"I sure don't want a mess," said Diane, stepping forward, rod out, as she made sure she had her hand positioned just right.

After checking her grip, Lew said, "Good. Now, your thumb is the key, because it adds punch to the cast." With that, she showed Diane how to make a roll cast.

After half an hour, all of which Lew had spent demonstrating and Diane following, they stepped out of the water to take a break.

"So this is what Bruce and Doc are doing as they fish upstream?" asked Diane.

"Yes, but the two of them are also trying to get better at the double haul, which has you using both a line hand and a hauling arm together. It's a rhythm that helps you cast further but also cast better in windy conditions. And it allows you to make more casts yet feel less fatigue because both your hands share the work. But, Diane, that's lesson for another day."

"Sign me up," said Diane with no hesitation.

"All right," said Lew, chortling. "One more thing, though. I want to talk to you about trout flies, because that's something people new to fly-fishing tend to go overboard on. The first thing to know is that trout flies are either wet or dry, depending on if you want the fish to see your trout fly on *top* of the water, acting like an insect they love that flies above or on the surface of the water. On the other hand, the wet fly mimics the insect that attracts the trout *under* the water."

"Sounds like I need a master's in insect science," said Diane.

"You just nailed the problem as I see it," said Lew. "Some fly fishermen get way too technical on the subject of trout flies. You'll see them wade into a trout stream with *hundreds* of the damn things stashed in their vests. Not me. I believe in simplicity.

"So one of my key rules is you should never carry more than five trout flies. Today I'll tell you my trout flies of choice, but as you learn more, you'll be able to make your own choices. It'll depend on where you're fishing and what insects may be flying or hatching or swimming at that time."

With that, Lew pulled a small plastic box from her fly-fishing vest and opened it to show Diane her choices. "Here I have one Royal Wulff, two tiny black-winged olives on number twenty-two and twenty-four hooks, respectively, a pale morning dun, and one salmon stone fly, which is a pretty outrageous little trout fly. On a day like today, these are my choices."

"I can see I have a lot to learn," said Diane. "How many lures does Ray use fishing muskies?"

"He has his favorites just like I have mine. One of the challenges and rewards of fly-fishing for me has always been watching to see what insect is hatching and what trout fly I can match to that to entice a trout." Lew gave Diane a big grin. "Diane, if you want a way to take your mind off work, off the problems in your life, off the problems in the world? Go fly-fishing.

"One more point I have to make today is that any trout you catch, you have to release. That is essential to this sport. People may keep and eat muskie, walleye, bass—but trout must be released."

"That I do know," said Diane as she got to her feet. "Okay, since the guys aren't back, I'll wade in and practice that roll cast." With that, she slid off the rock and into the stream.

Lew stayed where she was, happy to sit silent and watch. Off to her right, she saw something glint on the leaf of a nearby sumac. Sunlight on a dragonfly's wing: *heaven.*

* * *

As the sun went into hiding and the two men waded back to the clearing, Lew and Doc decided to enjoy the Friday fish fry at the Loon Lake Pub.

"We're hoping to finish work at the crime scene by late tomorrow morning," said Bruce. "Which means I'm here tonight, so count me in."

"And me? May I join you?" asked Diane in a shy voice.

"You're expected," said Lew, realizing the young grad student felt somewhat out of place. "If we get there in time, we can watch the six o'clock news and see how my press conference went. I'm hoping they show your photo enlarged and with all the color and detail included so that someone sees something that might help our investigation."

* * *

The Loon Lake Pub was packed, but they managed to get a table with a good view of one of the television screens and Osborne, who knew their waitress well, as she had been a patient, persuaded her to switch from ESPN sports to the local news. "Just the top stories will be fine," he said as he handed her a twenty-dollar bill.

"Doc, I'll pay you back," said Lew in whisper.

"Forget it, Lewellyn. My double haul was perfect this afternoon—at least the one time it worked." He grinned and patted her knee under the table.

The news came on. The three of them sat silent watching, even though the restaurant's buzz made it difficult to hear at times. It didn't matter. Lew could hear what she needed to hear. She was more concerned with the visuals during the broadcast.

After the news story was introduced, the reporter was shown asking "Sheriff Lew Ferris and Dr. Bruce Peters" several questions about the accidental death of Dr. Bert Willoughby and the apparent "nonaccidental" shooting that occurred two days later. Following a brief description of both victims, the reporter said, "It should be noted that both Dr. Willoughby and the late Robin Carpenter were expert pickleball players, which could prove to be a factor in their deaths. However, the authorities refused to comment on that."

The segment ended with the camera lingering on the enlarged photo from Diane's iPhone and a voice-over saying, "If anyone can identify the figure seen moving in this photo, please call the McBride County Sheriff's Department immediately."

Then the television returned to ESPN.

Lew glanced around the table, then watched her phone to see if it might light up with a call from dispatch. When, after five minutes had passed, nothing had happened, she sighed. "I'm sure we'll get a few nut calls, but I'm hoping . . ."

Though the fish fry, as usual, was very good, Lew had no appetite.

Chapter Twenty-Five

Exhausted after a very long day of cleaning for Jane Willoughby, Deb Wallace didn't have the energy to cook for herself. Instead, she put a frozen dinner in the oven and lay down to take a short nap while the food cooked. With the funeral scheduled for Tuesday and Jane's insistence on holding a wake for over a hundred people back at the house, Deb knew she'd be looking at another long day tomorrow.

When she woke from her nap, her food was ready. She set the plastic container on her television tray, settled into her ancient recliner, popped open a cold beer, and got ready to watch the six o'clock news. Paying halfhearted attention to the national news, she made a fruitless attempt to tackle the semifrozen spaghetti. Frustrated, she was walking toward the kitchen to put it back in the oven when she heard the reporter say something about Dr. Bert Willoughby. Deb stopped right where she was to watch the news report.

She wasn't surprised to hear law enforcement had confirmed the accidental shooting, but she was riveted when

the reporter said the sheriff's department was hoping someone could identify the "person of interest in the
following footage."

A series of photos showed an individual from the shoulders up and at a distance from the camera. What caught
Deb's eye wasn't the person—it was the color of the clothing the person was wearing: a bright, light blue. The color
was unusual and reminded her of the bright-blue color of
the hoodie she had found discarded in Jane's recycle bin.

Hmm, thought Deb as she walked into the kitchen to
give her dinner another twenty minutes in the oven. *Must
be the hot color this season.* She glanced over at the coat
hooks on the kitchen wall, where she had hung the hoodie,
hoping to wear it before the days got too cool. *Such a great
color.* She loved it.

* * *

After much back-and-forth with her mother that Friday,
Katherine finally agreed to stay over until after the funeral
and the wake on Tuesday. "Then I'm back to my own place,
Mom," she said. She didn't really mind staying over, but she
missed the quiet of her own home.

With her father out of the picture and Jane confident
that she was now one of the two primary beneficiaries of
Bert's estate, her mother had begun to behave as if she
might actually be happy. At least she wasn't stomping
around the house. That state of mind likely wouldn't last
long, Katherine knew. Jane wasn't really happy unless she
had something to get angry about.

Shortly before ten, Katherine settled onto the sofa in the family room to watch the ten o'clock news. She was curious to see what, if anything, might be reported about the death of Robin Carpenter. Jane had already retired to her own room, so Katherine turned up the volume on the newscast.

The report from the press conference at the sheriff's department opened with the news that her father's death had been ruled accidental. It moved on to the announcement of another shooting: "a tragic event that has taken the life of young woman, a native of Loon Lake." The reporter then segued into a "special announcement asking any resident who can identify the person of interest in the following photos to call the McBride County Sheriff's Department immediately."

Katherine was stunned. *Someone saw me?*

She stared at the photos, wishing she could hit a pause button, but it was television, not her laptop. What she saw was both disturbing and reassuring.

First, she saw herself moving beyond the trees and bushes, but her head and face were completely covered. The only identifying detail might be the color of the hooded sweatshirt she was wearing. *No*, Katherine said to herself, *that's ridiculous. Every time I turn around, I see women wearing hoodies that color. I even saw a woman wearing one at Walmart, for heaven's sake.*

An hour later, as she lay in bed, she came up with a plan, a plan as good as the one she'd had to get rid of Robin Carpenter, a plan that was so true to who she was and so smart that no one could ever second-guess her. And, what the heck, she probably wouldn't need it anyway.

Just as she had known the secret path to the old boys' camp grounds because of her friendship years ago with a grade school classmate who had lived near the road that ran behind the camp, Katherine had another memory from years past that would help her make a quick escape if she had to.

During her high school years, her father had insisted that Katherine and Jane join him to spend Labor Day weekends at a luxurious, private hunting lodge up north. Owned by one of his college friends who had made a fortune trading futures contracts, it was located just over the border in Ontario, Canada. Thanks to those dreary drives up through the Upper Peninsula of Michigan, Katherine knew how she could cross the border into Canada in four hours or less.

Besides, now that she knew the dental practice had been sold, she had no real reason to stay in Loon Lake. If she had to run, she would have the cash she'd found in Bert's desk drawer, and that would be more than enough to tide her over until she could arrange for her mom to send her money from the family inheritance. Jane might balk at first, put up a front of being appalled, but Katherine knew Jane. Her mother had to be very happy with how things had turned out. Especially happy that she would have sole control of the family trust with all its millions—and no Bert to stand in her way. *She can shop till she drops*, thought Katherine with a grim smile.

And, what the heck, if Katherine did find she needed to practice dentistry again, so what? Everywhere you went these days, dentists were in short supply, and no practice desperate for staff would be likely to run a background check on her credentials, much less run a criminal check.

Easy peasy, kiddo, Katherine told herself. This would be like running for prom queen all over again.

With that thought, she turned over and fell into a deep, sound sleep.

Chapter
Twenty-Six

Katherine woke to the sound of a garbage truck outside her bedroom window. *Oh, good*, she thought, remembering that Saturday mornings in her mother's neighborhood were when the recycling bins were picked up. That meant the hooded sweatshirt she had tucked down under the bags full of bottles and papers was long gone. The only evidence tying her to Robin Carpenter's death would soon be destroyed at the recycling plant.

As she swept the coverlet back to get up, she could hear her mother downstairs giving order after order to poor Deb. *Better Deb than me*, thought Katherine as she decided to get something to eat before heading off to the office to retrieve the cash in Bert's desk drawer.

* * *

Downstairs, Deb listened patiently as Jane went over a list of things she wanted done. "I want things to be perfect for when people are here Tuesday after the funeral service for Bert. I want to have a lovely, lovely wake," she said. "But,

Deb, did you forget I need a new ostrich feather duster for my Mings?"

"No, I did not forget," said Deb, walking back to the kitchen, where she had set the box with the new feather duster on the floor near the coatrack. She reached for a box cutter to slice open the box, grabbed the long-handled feather duster, and walked back into Jane's small den to hand it to her.

"It wasn't cheap, Mrs. Willoughby," said Deb as she handed it over, "but I assumed you wanted it regardless. Cost was seventeen dollars. Hope that's okay."

"Fine, fine," said Jane, barely listening. "Just set it in the corner there. I'll get to my Mings later."

Deb waited, hoping Jane would hand her some cash from her purse. After a short wait, she realized the woman's head was elsewhere. She'd ask her later.

Turning to go back to the kitchen, she glanced into the room holding Bert's gun collection. She paused, turned back to Jane, and asked, "Was that you who took the Browning off the gun rack the other day? Shouldn't I be dusting all these before people come for the wake?"

"The Browning? You mean the rifle? Good god, Deb. I haven't touched a gun in thirty years. Of course it wasn't me. But thank you for reminding me. Yes, would you mind dusting all those? I'm hoping one of Bert's buddies will take an interest in that collection. I would love to get it off my hands. That room would make a lovely sitting room, don't you think?"

Back in the kitchen, Deb puzzled over that Browning rifle. There was no doubt it had been missing when she arrived early Thursday morning. Was it Katherine who had taken it? Had to be. No one else had been in the house. At least not that she was aware of. Maybe the evening before?

As she reached for the mop in the back hall, she paused. She had a sudden memory of walking into the garage with a sack full of empty bottles, opening the recycle bin, and seeing the hint of bright-blue fabric peeking out from below other bags of trash. Now that she thought of it, that hadn't been there earlier in the week when she had put trash in the bin, or she would certainly have seen it then. Plus neither Jane nor Katherine was known to ever lift a hand to clean or pick something up. One of those two had to have gone out of their way to shove the blue hoodie down and under. The more Deb thought about it, the more she realized: *someone had intended to hide that hoodie.*

Deb tensed. She decided there was one phone call she better make right away. *Don't jump to conclusions*, she told herself. *You could be wrong. Get a grip, girl.*

* * *

As Katherine walked out of the upstairs hall bathroom after brushing her teeth, she heard Deb ask Jane about the Browning rifle. Not a good sign. Back in the bedroom, she reached into the bottom drawer of the dresser that had been hers since childhood. She opened the small wooden box that her late grandfather, Bert's father, had given her on her thirteenth birthday.

"Every woman needs to know how to shoot a gun," the old man had said as he handed her the .22 pistol. Then he had driven her out to a clearing in the county forest where targets had been set up by hunters sighting their guns. Over the next two hours, he had taught her how to load the pistol, handle it safely, and shoot. When time after time she was able to hit the target, he was so pleased that it made her happy. They were pals, those two, and Katherine had missed him over the years. Unlike her father, that old man had liked her.

She tucked the pistol and extra bullets into her purse, planning ahead in case she had to drive north. After hurrying down the oak staircase, she grabbed a banana off the kitchen counter and headed into the garage.

* * *

Meeting with Judith and Dani in her office, Lew went over the list of tips they had received after the evening news had showcased the unknown person caught by Diane Knutsen's phone. The list was short and disappointing.

"Doesn't look promising," said Lew after scrolling through the memo Judith had emailed her earlier.

"No," said Dani, "and the few I picked up off the internet were obvious pranksters or nutcases."

"I called the television stations a short time ago," said Judith, "and asked if they would agree to run the story on their noon news shows today. I was hoping they would do it one more time."

"They agreed?" asked Lew.

"Not only that—they will post the story and the photo on their websites too."

"Okay," said Lew, exhaling, "then we wait. The Wausau boys have the bullets that killed Robin Carpenter, so if we get any leads, they're confident the ballistics team can determine if there's a match. But . . ." She paused.

"I know," said Judith, sounding frustrated, "we need a gun."

"Or a fashion statement," said Dani. "That's a pretty distinctive color that person was wearing. Maybe a female viewer will pick up on that."

Their morning meeting ended just as Osborne walked in for his daily cup of coffee with Lew. "Thank you, Doc," said Lew as he filled her coffee mug, "I need *something* positive this morning."

* * *

Katherine pulled into a parking spot in front of the old bank building that housed the Willoughby dental practice. She usually parked behind the building, but this morning she planned to run in and out without taking the time to go in the back way and fuss with the building keys. The front door on the street side opened to a stairwell leading up past offices belonging to lawyers and an accountant, so that door was always open. Katherine ran up the stairs to her office.

The elegant old brick building dated back to 1894. Her great-grandfather, the first dentist in the Willoughby family, had opened his practice up on the second floor of the bank building in 1926. Ever since then, the Willoughbys had owned the entire back of the old building: the large waiting room for patients, three rooms with dental chairs, two offices, and a back room for relaxing.

Off the back room was a large closet that her great-grandfather had converted into what he called "the gold room." There he kept the gold and mercury, metals used for fillings in those days. One tempted burglars; the other could be toxic.

The closet was outfitted with wooden shelves for the containers holding the metals, two straight-backed chairs to use when working with the metals, a stepladder, and a heavy wooden door. The door's brass lock could be opened only from the outside with an antique brass key that hung on a hook near the entrance to the back room, hidden under an old black umbrella.

*   *   *

At the door to Willoughby Dental, Katherine inserted her key and walked in. To her surprise, Robin Steadman was seated at the receptionist's desk, head bent over the appointments book. She was dressed casually in jeans and a long-sleeved navy-blue shirt, obviously ready for the weekend.

"Oh, Robin," said Katherine in surprise. "What are you doing here? Aren't you off on Saturday?"

Robin looked up at her with a smile. "I usually am, but with your dad's funeral on Tuesday, I need to finish moving some of these appointments for you and the hygienist. Sue Ellen usually worked Tuesdays," she said, referring to the hygienist, "so I remembered in the middle of the night last night that I have her appointments to change too." She smiled as she gave a sigh of exasperation. "Also, we have the cleaning crew in either this afternoon or tomorrow morning, so I'm putting a few things away before they get here. Do you need anything?"

"No, just picking up a few more things from Dad's office. I'll be out of here in a minute."

"Okay," said Robin, getting to her feet. "I'll be in Sue Ellen's room if you need anything. And I'm leaving my cell phone here by the appointments book, so don't be surprised if you hear it ringing. I keep it on speaker so I can hear who's calling."

"Got it. See you Tuesday, then," said Katherine as she headed toward Bert's office.

Once there, she unlocked the desk drawer and reached in for the cash. *Whoa*, she thought when she found three stacks. The day before she had assumed there were only the two stacks she had seen when she pulled the drawer open. She took a few minutes to take a closer look through the money before thrusting it all into her purse. Each small stack of hundred-dollar bills, held together with rubber bands, appeared to add up to at least ten thousand dollars. Thirty thousand dollars? This was much better than she had expected.

She heard Robin's cell phone ring, and since Robin had left the phone on speaker, a familiar voice could be heard. Katherine walked over to the door and cracked it open so she could hear better. "Robin?" Katherine heard Deb's voice on speakerphone. "This is Deb Wallace. Are you there?"

Katherine heard Robin run out to the desk and pick up. "Yes, Deb, here I am. Need an appointment? . . . What? No, I haven't been by the Willoughbys' since before Bert was killed. What? . . . No, I certainly did not borrow that gun. Sorry. Do I know who did? Hold on a minute, I . . ."

* * *

Katherine was surprised at how easy it was to knock the woman unconscious. She hit her once with the butt of the pistol, expecting a struggle. That Robin went down so easy was a relief. Then Katherine picked up the cell phone that Robin had dropped and turned it off. After turning Robin onto her back, Katherine grabbed her by both shoulders and dragged her body down the long hallway to the back room.

Once there, she pulled Robin into the gold room and left her lying flat on her back. With no windows, no phone, and a solid door locked shut from the outside, Robin wouldn't be able to alert anyone for hours, maybe not until Sunday when the cleaning crew arrived.

Before Katherine locked the gold room door, she bent over to be sure the woman was alive. She was, but still unconscious. Katherine didn't see any blood, so that was good. Robin Steadman was not Robin Carpenter. Robin Steadman had only ever been helpful—she didn't need to die.

As Katherine ran down the stairs and out of the bank building, she stopped at a city trash container two doors down and threw the brass key to the gold room into the trash. A minute later, she was in her car speeding to her mother's house.

Once there, she parked in the back and crept in through the back door to the kitchen, worried she might see Deb, but there was no sign of her. She crept down the hallway and past her mother's small office. Jane was there, her back to the open hall door and busy chatting with someone on the phone.

So far so good, thought Katherine as she crept up the wooden stairs to the second floor. Once in her bedroom undetected, she acted quickly and silently, determined to avoid alerting Deb and Jane. She grabbed her backpack and jammed in a few clothes, her iPad, her toothbrush, and her chargers. Then back down the stairs she crept. Jane was still chatting. Deb must be down in the laundry room.

Back in the driveway and about to throw her backpack in her SUV, she made another quick decision. She backed her father's silver Mercedes out of the three-car garage and pulled her SUV into his space.

Good, she thought. If any cops or state troopers came after her, they might not think to look for her father's car. All she needed was four hours and she would be safe. Safe in Canada, safe to start life over the way she wanted it. *Good*, she thought again, *just keep your eyes on the road*. As she drove out of Loon Lake, she remembered to power down her iPhone.

No tracking that either, she thought with satisfaction as she thrust the phone into her purse.

Chapter
Twenty-Seven

Deb was standing in the back room off the kitchen talking to Robin Steadman when their conversation stopped unexpectedly. For a moment or two, Deb heard nothing, then the sound of scuffling before Robin's phone went dead.

Deb waited, hoping for a callback, but nothing happened. *Hold on*, she told herself. After all, she was calling on a Saturday morning, and she might have caught Robin Steadman driving somewhere or outdoors where there was a gap in cell service.

She waited. Nothing.

After five minutes had gone by, she decided to try Robin Steadman's cell number again. She had closed the door to the kitchen and hoped Jane wouldn't walk in. She didn't want to have the conversation where her employer might hear her.

After one more try and still no answer, she decided to wait half an hour and try her once more. If she didn't answer then . . .

The half hour passed slowly, but Deb knew that if she couldn't reach Robin Steadman one more time to confirm that it must be Katherine who had moved that Browning rifle, she would have to call the police, despite knowing that even if she was wrong, just making the call would mark the end of her working for Jane Willoughby.

After changing the laundry, emptying the dishwasher, and cleaning the guest bathroom, she decided to give Robin Steadman one last try. Still no answer.

Okay. Deb steeled herself. She had to make the call. It would change her life, but she knew she had to do it.

* * *

"I think I know who killed that woman at the boys' camp—"

She was explaining when the woman on dispatch who had answered her call interrupted to say, "Please hold. I'm putting you through to Sheriff Ferris' office."

Deb waited for less than ten seconds before the line was answered.

"Hello, this is Judith Hanson in the McBride County Sheriff's Department, and I understand you have information on the fatal shooting at the boys' camp? May I have your name, please?"

Deb told her who she was and said, "Katherine Willoughby is the person you want—"

"Hold on," said Judith, "Sheriff Ferris needs to hear you. Please stay on the line while I put you though to her."

Again it took less than a few seconds, and Deb heard a woman's voice. "Hello, Deb Wallace? This is Sheriff Ferris. Please tell me what you know."

"Yes," said Deb. "I work for the Willoughby family—I'm their housekeeper, and two things have happened here at the house. Yesterday, one of Dr. Willoughby's guns was missing. He has a collection, but there's only one gun that's ever used by anyone, and that Browning rifle was not on the rack yesterday morning—"

"Someone stole it?"

"No! Today it's back. It's here, but it was missing when I came in yesterday morning around six thirty. I've cleaned here ten years, Sheriff. I know that room and those guns."

"Okay. I need that gun, but please don't touch it until I get there."

"I understand, but one more thing. I have a blue hoodie sweatshirt just like the one shown on the news last night. I found it in the trash here—"

"Deb, are you safe?" asked Lew, getting to her feet.

"Yes, I'm sitting outside in my car."

"Where? At your home?"

"No. I'm parked at the back of the Willoughby house to the right of their garage."

"Is Katherine Willoughby there?"

Deb looked off to her left. The garage door to the stall where Katherine kept her SUV was empty. "No, I don't see her car. She's been staying here since Bert was killed. Maybe she's over at her condo?"

"Please stay right where you are—in your car with the doors locked—until we arrive."

* * *

Off the phone and working as fast as she could, Lew arranged for a search warrant of the Willoughby home. After receiving it, she signaled for two deputies to follow her in their squad cars and alerted Judith, saying, "Ask Dani to find the license number for Katherine Willoughby's car. I'm going to the Willoughby residence, where she's been staying, but I want to be ready if we need to put out an APB."

"Do you want an APB out now?" asked Judith.

"No. Let me confirm what Deb Wallace told me first."

Judith nodded.

"Also, please find the address of Katherine's condo and ask two deputies to check to see if her car is there. If it is, tell them to park nearby and wait for my arrival. If she leaves, call me ASAP. If she isn't there, tell them to stay at that location until I say otherwise. She could show up there. We need to be prepared."

"Prepared for what?" asked Judith.

Lew gave her a level look as she said, "You never know what people will do. If Deb Wallace is right, this woman is dangerous."

* * *

Lew parked in front of the large Willoughby home and motioned for one of the deputies to follow behind her while she sent the other to check on Deb Wallace and escort her to Lew's office back at the sheriff's department. Then she walked up to the front door and knocked.

"Who's there?" a woman's voice called out from inside. No one came to the door.

Lew knocked again.

"Oh, stop it, I'm coming," said a cross voice as the door was yanked open. Jane Willoughby peered over the rim of her glasses, irritation mixed with surprise flooding her flat round face. "What do *you* want?" she demanded.

"I'd like to speak to your daughter, Katherine. Is she here?"

Looking back over her left shoulder, Jane hollered, "Katherine—get down here. You have company." She waited. Lew waited. Nothing. Jane turned sideways, threw her spidery arms up in frustration, and hollered again, aiming her voice up the stairway behind her. "Katherine. Dammit. Get down here now."

Again, nothing.

"Mrs. Willoughby, do you have any idea where your daughter might be?"

"I thought she was upstairs. Apparently not."

"Mrs. Willoughby, I have a warrant to search your home, specifically the room containing your late husband's guns. May I please come in?"

Without saying a word but looking puzzled, Jane held the door open for Lew to enter. As Lew walked into the house, she motioned for the deputies to follow her. She walked across the hallway to where she could see a wall of gun racks. As she walked up close to the racks immediately in front of her, she spotted a Browning rifle anchoring one end of the nearest rack.

"Is this the gun that your husband used for rabbits?" asked Lew, pointing to the Browning. "This is the gun you thought had been used to shoot your husband, correct?"

"Yes. That's the only one Bert ever let anybody touch. The rest of these guns are worth thousands—"

She apparently was ready to extoll the virtues of the collection, but Lew cut her off, saying, "Thank you. We need the Browning for evidence." With that, she directed one of the deputies to secure the gun. "This will be returned to you once we've completed our investigation." After the deputies had walked out with the rifle, Lew said, "Mrs. Willoughby, we need to find your daughter. Please let us know if you hear anything from her." Jane's eyes widened.

"I can't say more at the moment," said Lew. "Meanwhile, don't be alarmed when you see me drive around to the back of your house."

"What? Why?" asked Jane, confused.

"We'll let you know when we know more," said Lew. "Right now we need to find your daughter."

As Lew left, Jane stood speechless.

*   *   *

Back in her cruiser, Lew's cell phone rang. "Lew, Barbara Steadman is on the line," said Judith. "She is worried—she hasn't been able to reach her daughter. She wants to talk to you."

"Put her on," said Lew as she pulled onto the street heading toward her office. She knew Barbara wouldn't be calling without a good reason.

"Lewellyn, something is wrong," said Barbara Steadman. "I've been trying to reach Robin for the last two hours, and I get no answer. I know something's wrong."

The tone in her old friend's voice convinced Lew she was right. There was worry, and then there was the conviction that comes from the gut. Barbara was right: something *was* wrong.

"Okay, Barbara. We're searching for the woman she works for too—"

"Go by Robin's house," Barbara said, interrupting. "That's where she was when we talked last. Maybe something happened there."

Lew clicked off and headed toward the small house where she knew Robin Steadman lived. She pulled over to the curb in front of the small brown-shingled house. It had a cheery white front porch that held two rattan rocking chairs. Lew ran up a small set of concrete stairs to knock on the porch door. No answer. She ran down the stairs and onto a short driveway that led toward the back of the house and a small garden. At the back side door that she knew opened to the kitchen, Lew knocked hard. No answer.

"Say there, looking for Robin?" called a voice from behind her. Lew turned to see a short gray-haired woman in jeans and a red T-shirt holding grass clippers in one hand. She was standing on the other side of the driveway.

"Yes. Have you seen her?"

"Yeah—an hour ago. She was walking to work. I was surprised she was going in on a Saturday, but she said she had paperwork. I wouldn't worry if I were you. Robin's a hard worker. I'll bet you can find her home this afternoon."

"Thank you," said Lew, managing a smile. She ran back to the cruiser, jumped in, and headed for the dental office. While she was driving, she checked in with Judith. "Any news on Katherine Willoughby?"

"We have her license number, and Deb Wallace is here. Also, Deputy Warren checked in to say no sign of Katherine or her car at her condo. What do you want me to do?"

"Put out the APB. I'm heading for the dental office, where Robin Steadman hasn't been answering her phone. Her mother is very worried . . . I'm very worried."

"Shall I send someone over?"

Lew thought for one instant before saying, "Yes. Let's hope Barbara and I are overreacting."

* * *

Less than five minutes later, Lew pulled up in front of the bank building where she knew Bert Willoughby had his offices. She hurried up the stairs, past the lawyer and accountant offices, to the door marked WILLOUGHBY DEN-TAL. The office space on the other side of the door appeared to be dark.

Assuming the dental office was closed for Saturday and the door was locked, Lew knocked. When she heard no answer, she tried the knob. To her surprise, it was unlocked. She opened the door and peered in. She found herself staring down a dark front hall with a darkened waiting room off to the right. Just to be sure Robin wasn't there, she stepped into the hall, calling, "Robin? Robin, it's Lew Ferris. Anyone here?"

No answer.

Looking around as she walked into the hall and past the receptionist's desk, Lew spotted the edge of something black on the floor to one side of the desk. Walking around the desk, she found an iPhone lying on the floor near the desk chair, and off to the other side of the chair was a woman's purse.

Checking the phone first, she saw that it had been powered down. She reached for the wallet in the purse. It was Robin Steadman's. The phone had to be hers too. Holding the iPhone, Lew pressed the side and volume buttons to power it back on. As she did so, the phone lit up with a call. She saw Barbara's name on the screen and answered. "I'm here, Barbara, but—"

Before she could say more, she heard a series of thuds from the far end of the hall. Holding the phone in one hand, she ran down the hall in the direction of the muted thuds.

"Hold on, Barbara," said Lew. "I hear something. Call you right back." Clicking the phone off, she shoved it into her back pocket.

At the end of the hall, Lew found herself in a small room. Two easy chairs with footstools faced windows opening to the street below. A coffeemaker and a basket of paper napkins were on a small table near a sink holding used coffee mugs. Copies of magazines and newspapers made it obvious this was the office break room.

Turning in a circle, she heard the sound again, louder now—a pounding against what must be a closet door. Before Lew could say anything, she heard a muffled woman's voice call out, "Help. Help, please. I'm locked in here."

"Is that you, Robin?" asked Lew, trying the doorknob.

"Yes, help me out of here, please." Lew could hear Robin start to cry.

Lew tried the door again. "It's locked. Where's the key?"

"On the wall above the coffeemaker. Under that umbrella," called Robin through her sobs.

Lew grabbed the umbrella to look underneath it. She saw an empty hook. "Nothing here."

Lew walked over to the door. The closet's wooden door with its brass keyhole had to date back to the original building. "Robin, is there room for you to stand back and off to one side? I'm going to see if I can shoot through this lock." She had her Sig Sauer ready.

"Yes, please get me out of here."

Lew pulled the trigger.

The doorframe around the lock shattered, and the lock released. Lew pulled the door open to find Robin collapsed on one of the chairs, blood trickling down the left side of her head and neck. The yellow T-shirt she was wearing was dotted with blood. Lew called for an ambulance.

With one arm under Robin's shoulders, Lew helped her out of the closet and into one of the easy chairs near the windows. She grabbed a handful of the paper napkins and held them against the back of Robin's head.

"I'm okay, really," Robin managed. "My head really hurts, though."

"Yeah, well, you're not okay," said Lew, "but you're not dead, thank god. I have to call your mother right now." And she punched in Barbara's number.

"She's alive, Barbara. Looks to me like she took a blow to her head that knocked her unconscious, but she appears okay otherwise. Ambulance is on its way. Call you back once we have her on the way to the emergency room at St. Mary's." And she clicked off.

As they waited for the ambulance crew, she said, "Robin, I have to ask, even though I'm sure I know the answer: Who did this to you?"

Robin gave her a sideways look. "Katherine, I think. She was here, then I . . . she must have hit me from behind. Why, I have no idea."

"When was that? Have you any idea?"

"Yes, just ten minutes after nine. I was on the phone. Deb Wallace called me, and that's all I remember . . ."

Lew checked her watch. It was twenty minutes after one.

Chapter
Twenty-Eight

The report from the Wausau Crime Lab came in at 3:20 that afternoon: the bullets that had killed Robin Carpenter matched the Browning rifle from the Willoughby home. The unused cartridges found on the path near where Diane Knutsen was hiding had fingerprints that matched prints found on the rifle.

Though Katherine Willoughby had never been fingerprinted, Lew and Bruce Peters agreed the prints had to be hers. They would wait until she was arrested to confirm the matches.

In the meantime, Deb Wallace had retrieved the blue hoodie from her home. "The good news," she told Lew, Dani, and Judith, who were examining it together, "is that I haven't had a chance to launder it. This is the condition I found it in."

"The color is right," said Dani, holding it near the enlarged photo of the runner that she had brought up on her computer screen.

"It is," agreed Lew and Judith, both nodding. With that, Lew placed it in an evidence bag. "We'll let the Wausau boys check for DNA."

* * *

Katherine watched the blue dot on the navigation screen in her father's Mercedes. She was a good three hours into Upper Michigan, and there had been no sign of any state troopers or local police signaling for her to pull over. She continued to think her decision to take Bert's car had been brilliant.

What was bothering her now was the thought of all the money her mother would have access to and that she would need herself. Could she persuade her mother to come through for her? Jane could go ballistic over the smallest things.

Stop it! Katherine told herself. *Don't think that way.* She reminded herself that Jane had come through for her before and, while it might take a few months, she was sure to come through for her again. *Yes*, thought Katherine, *Mom will totally understand why I had to leave the country. I know she will.*

A sign for Escanaba caught her eye. Whoa. Getting close. Only a couple more hours, and she would be home free. Well, kinda. An hour ago, while using the restroom in the gas station, she had counted the cash from Bert's drawer: seventy-three thousand dollars. That would be get her through at least six months.

As she was passing a slow car, she realized she had forgotten something important. Very important. Her passport. *Goddammit.* She had traveled to Mexico with her parents over the holidays, and her mother, always OCD when it came to international travel, had insisted on keeping the family's passports "in one safe place." With no plans of her own to travel internationally since then, Katherine hadn't objected, but she'd forgotten to claim her passport once she was back in her condo.

She took the next exit, turned left at the top of the ramp, and got back on the highway headed south toward Loon Lake. *No problem*, she assured herself. Yes, it would delay her escape, but it couldn't be helped. With this car, she would be able to slip into town and into her mother's house easy. She knew right where the passport was; Jane kept all three of their passports, along with her jewelry—"the pearls from my mother that are worth thousands, you know"—in a drawer in her dressing table. In the same drawer where her mother hid the small leather jewelry case, Katherine knew she would find the passports hidden behind tubes of face cream. Not in Jane's den on the first floor, but up in the bedroom she had shared with Bert.

All Katherine had to do was run upstairs and grab it.

* * *

By four o'clock that day, Jane Willoughby realized she really had lost her housekeeper. Deb hadn't returned to help with all the cleaning Jane wanted done before the wake on Tuesday. She hadn't answered the half dozen calls Jane had made to her cell phone either.

She decided to go ahead to the florist's rather than wait any longer for Deb to show up. Pulling on a jacket, she started out to the garage and her car. When she hit the button to open the garage door for her car, she was surprised to see Bert's Mercedes gone and Katherine's SUV parked in his space.

Her first thought was that the beautiful car had been stolen. Her second thought was the realization Katherine had taken Bert's car. It was the first moment she had allowed herself to face what her daughter had done. Fact: she must have killed the woman with whom her father had been having an illicit affair and to whom he had left all his money. *Who could blame her for that?* Jane could understand her daughter's thinking, but her actions? That Katherine would go to such an extreme was shocking.

It also puzzled Jane that Katherine had done something to hurt Robin Steadman. After all, Bert had left a very small amount of money to that young woman. And Robin had been such a help to him. For heaven's sake, she deserved the money. Why on earth would Katherine have hurt her?

Jane pondered the missing car. She wouldn't be surprised if Katherine had decided to make a new life in Canada. That could work. Jane knew her daughter had no close friends in Loon Lake. Actually, she had never had close friends in Loon Lake, ever. That wasn't Katherine. She was independent.

If she *was* in Canada, that meant she would be fine. No prison, and Jane could always visit. Visit and share some of what Bert had left her now that the unpleasant woman was out of the picture. Although maybe she was wrong about that. Canadian authorities might restrict her travel if they knew she was related to a fugitive. Hmm, she would have to figure something out. Maybe Katherine already had a plan.

Jane got into her car and headed off to the florist. That Bert's car was missing was no one's business.

When she arrived, the florist has the flowers waiting. Fifteen minutes later, she was home and Bert's car was still missing.

Chapter Twenty-Nine

Katherine drove down the driveway to the back of her parents' house. She parked and let herself in through the back door leading to the kitchen. Once inside, she was relieved to find the kitchen empty. At first, she wondered where Deb was, as the woman was usually there cleaning or cooking.

She tiptoed down the hall to the oak stairway and looked up. Her mother was busy doing something in the sitting area on the landing between the bedrooms. Katherine inched her way up the stairs, determined to make as little noise as possible and hoping Deb wouldn't suddenly appear at the bottom of the stairs, spot her, and say something.

Even as she neared the top stairs, Jane remained oblivious to her approach. Katherine could see why. Her mother was standing on the third rung of a stepladder she had set up. She had a long-handled feather duster in her right hand and was reaching over the top of the antique armoire to dust each of her precious Ming vases.

Moving slowly and taking care not to make a sound, Katherine got to the top of the stairwell, crept across the Oriental carpet, keeping to the left of where Jane was standing on her stepladder, and slipped through the open door into her mother's bedroom. She headed straight for the dressing table, slid the drawer open slowly so it wouldn't squeak, and reached in. Alongside the small black leather jewelry case her mother carried when traveling were the passports. Three of them. Katherine opened the first—Bert's. She opened the second—hers. *Thank goodness.*

Cautiously, she slid the drawer closed, then crept to the bedroom door. She tiptoed across the landing, keeping to the right of her mother, who was still standing with her right arm extended up and over so she could dust the farthest away of the three Ming vases. Katherine got to the edge of the top stair at the same moment that, from the corner of her eye, her mother caught sight of movement.

"Katherine!" exclaimed Jane, sweeping her right arm back in surprise. The feather duster caught Katherine full in the face. She staggered back, her heel catching in the edge of the Oriental rug. Twisting as she tried to keep her balance, she stumbled sideways, only to fall forward.

Jane watched in stunned silence as her daughter plunged headfirst down the elegant oak staircase.

The EMTs arrived within minutes, but Katherine was unresponsive. An autopsy showed a fractured vertebra had severed her spinal cord, killing her instantly.

They found Katherine's passport on the eighth step, where it must have dropped as she fell.

Chapter Thirty

～

Lew gazed out across the lake as the sun was setting over the pale-gold tamaracks hugging the far shore. Close to where she was sitting on Ray's dock, the leaves of a white oak were turning amber and rust, another colorful reminder that winter was soon to arrive.

She turned her attention back to the young woman sitting next to her on the bench. "I need advice," said Diane Knutsen, her tone apologetic. "I know this isn't a major life decision like marriage or something, but I don't want to hurt anyone's feelings—"

Before she could say more, Osborne stepped up onto the dock after walking down from his home.

"Diane is trying to decide if she should go fishing with Ray," said Lew, looking at Osborne. "He wants to show her how to cast a spinning rod and teach her how to fish muskie. Her confusion is my fault. I encouraged her to learn fly-fishing first. But she's finding it hard to say no to Ray."

"It's so nice of him to offer," said Diane.

What went unspoken was something Lew and Osborne knew well: no doubt Diane, like so many young women before her, found Ray too good-looking, too entertaining, and too endearing to turn down. Problem was, Ray Pradt most likely was not a good long-term investment. Commitment was not high on Ray's list of priorities.

Yet he was *the* expert on how to fish muskies, the best teacher Diane was likely to meet.

"I'm already a little overwhelmed between wet flies, dry flies, streamers, lures, jigs—all this fishing lingo," said Diane with a laugh. "I made the mistake of looking up some trout and muskie websites before I fell asleep last night. So forget spinning rods—my *head* is spinning."

Lew looked across the dock to where Ray was busy getting his boat ready to take Diane out for her first lesson. She had to make a decision.

Lew turned to Osborne, saying, "What's your opinion, Doc?"

"I would encourage you to go out with Ray this evening, but be frank with him that you're trying to decide between learning to fly-fish or fish muskies," said Osborne. "And here's why. I grew up fishing with a spinning rod, whether for muskie or walleye or bluegills—years of bait fishing. And it has not been easy for me to make the transition from casting a spinning rod to casting a fly rod. Now, that said, I know you're attracted to our friend here . . ."

Ohmygod, thought Lew as she listened to Osborne, *it is so much better for Doc to be saying this than me. I owe him.* She grinned as Osborne kept talking.

"But Ray will understand if you decide muskie fishing isn't for you. At least not right now, when"—Osborne paused to wink at Lew—"you have a chance to learn fly-fishing from one of the finest instructors in the Northwoods."

"You think he'll understand?" asked Diane.

"Let me put it this way, Diane," said Lew. "Ray is a fanatic outdoors guy—"

"That's me too," Diane interrupted her. "I'm a fanatic for the outdoors too."

"That's our point exactly," said Lew, looking to Osborne for support. "It isn't just muskie fishing that the two of you might enjoy together. It's the entire outdoors universe. Right, Doc?"

"He already told me he's hoping you'll show him your research on ruffed grouse. You two may have more in common that a couple of fish," said Osborne with a smile.

Diane smiled back. "So what do I do now? Tell him I don't want to go and take this lesson tonight?"

"Gosh, no," said Lew. "You should go and pay attention to what he shows you. Try your best so you can learn the differences. That will make it easy for Ray to understand when you say you prefer to start with one over the other—at this time."

"And keep an open mind," said Osborne. "Who's to say you won't find that you prefer fishing for the big girls, the muskies?"

"So what exactly should I pay attention to?" asked Diane.

"It's pretty simple," said Lew. "The key difference is in the casting technique. Standing in a boat and casting with a spinning rod means using your casting arm in a way quite different from casting a fly rod. When you cast a spinning rod, you use your elbow as a fulcrum moving sideways. Like this." Lew got to her feet to show Diane what she meant.

"But when you cast a fly rod, it's your *grip* that is critical. That's because you use your thumb to add punch to the cast. And when you cast, you keep your wrist straight and your forearm in line with your upper arm. That means your elbow is in line with your shoulder." Lew moved her arm so Diane could see the difference.

"So casting with a fly rod is different from casting with a spinning rod. But keep in mind that when you fly-fish, unless you're on the ocean, you're fishing for a small fish, not a forty-four-inch behemoth. And you're standing in maybe a foot of water in a trout stream—not on an eighteen-foot fishing boat over water eighty feet deep. Two very different experiences. So wait and see how you feel after your time with Ray tonight," said Lew. "It's your choice, and I'll be here next summer." As a lanky figure wearing a stuffed walleye on his head sauntered over to join them on the dock, she said, "Oops, look who's got his boat ready to go."

"Hey, guys, why do frogs want to be rappers?" asked Ray as he held out a hand to help Diane step off the dock. With a grin at Lew and Doc and before they could groan, he answered his own question: "Because they are big into hip-hop. Ready to go, Miss Knutsen?"

"You've been warned, Diane," said Lew, chortling as the two left the dock and walked toward Ray's boat. Diane turned and waved, a big smile on her face.

Lew got to her feet. "Come on, Doc, it's early. Let's take a short walk before we call it a day."

* * *

At the top of the lane that led down to Ray's trailer home, Lew turned and said, "Go right or left? You choose, Doc."

"I say go left," said Osborne, nudging her gently by the elbow as he walked beside her along Loon Lake Road. They headed off in the direction of the old boys' camp.

Half a mile down the road, Lew said, "Let's not go all the way to the boys' camp. I need fresh air, but I don't need to be reminded of the paperwork waiting for me. Thanks to the resolution of the Willoughby-Carpenter case, I have one very busy week coming up. And that, Doc, is the only drawback to being sheriff over an entire county—too much of it is a desk job."

"You got the reports from Bruce and the Wausau boys, right?" asked Osborne. "No question it was Katherine who shot Robin Carpenter?"

"Yes, the crime lab ballistics experts have confirmed that the bullets that killed Robin Carpenter matched the Willoughbys' Browning rifle. We also got a DNA match to Katherine Willoughby on that blue hooded sweatshirt. And, Doc, I want to thank you again for encouraging Bob Portman to call me."

"What did he say exactly, Lew? I know he was shocked to hear the news about Katherine and Robin Carpenter when he got back from that fishing trip."

"He didn't say much, only that after Jane Willoughby had bullied him into telling her the contents of Bert's will and Bert's plan to divorce her that he would've bet it was Jane who went after the Carpenter woman—not Katherine." She paused. "He added he had too much trust in human beings. It never dawned on him that one of those two women would actually commit murder. As he talked, I could tell Bob feels some responsibility for what happened."

"He shouldn't," said Osborne. "All he did was follow his client's wishes. He was never in a position to second-guess the actions of a disturbed personality."

"I know what you mean. I keep learning how people can surprise you. Take Jane Willoughby. The time I spent with her that night after Katherine's death? She was the primary witness, so I had to get her statement as soon as possible, and being around the woman was downright strange."

"I imagine she was hysterical," said Osborne.

"Right? That's what I was expecting, but she was quite the opposite. She struck me as too calm, too quiet— almost . . . peaceful. I know I'm being unkind when I say this, but she seemed almost *satisfied*. Gave me the creeps, Doc. It was like she was happy how everything had turned out, so happy it felt, at least to me"—Lew pressed her right hand against her chest—"*evil*. I know that sounds extreme, but that's how it felt.

"I keep wondering, too, why she didn't alert us when she found her husband's car missing. If we had been able to put out the APB for the license plate on that car, I'm sure we would have caught Katherine within hours of her leaving town and certainly when she drove back."

"You couldn't track her cell phone either?" asked Osborne.

"She had powered it off, so all Dani could find was the last location where it had been used—and that was Jane's house. So if Jane had alerted us that Katherine was driving Bert Willoughby's car, then her daughter might still be alive. We could have arrested her hours before she fell down those stairs . . ." Lew shook her head. "So sad."

Again Lew and Osborne walked in silence, Lew going over and over in her mind what she might have done differently so that Katherine Willoughby would still be alive.

"I called Barbara Steadman yesterday," said Lew after a few minutes. "I wanted to know how her Robin is doing, and I mentioned to Barbara what I thought about Jane's behavior."

"And what did she say?"

"She said that, based on what her daughter has told her over the years while she's been working in Bert's dental office, she—Barbara—isn't surprised. 'Those two fought all the time, so with Bert gone, the source of Jane's anger is gone.' That was Barbara's comment.

"And Barbara said too that Robin never got the impression that Jane and Katherine were close, and now, with Katherine gone, Jane doesn't have to share those millions. Barbara thinks the woman has to be happy—even if she tries to hide it."

"Bob Portman told me that Robin Carpenter's family is challenging the will," said Osborne. "Even though Bert may have insisted on the trust reverting to the Willoughby family in the event of Robin's death, Bob isn't sure that will hold up in court. So Jane may inherit the assets earned after her marriage to Bert but not the monies in the trust. She's still well off no matter what, however."

On they walked under the darkening sky. Owls hooted, and Lew heard rustling in the bushes along the road. Rabbits?

The sound reminded her of the young boy who had accidentally shot Bert Willoughby. "Doc, you know how I have been worried about that young Danny who shot the rifle that killed Bert."

"Any news on the youngster?"

"Yes, I spoke with Lillian Herman with youth services today, and she had some good news. A couple, both college professors who have been unable to have children, are committed to long-term care of Danny—and very interested in possibly adopting him if his father loses or relinquishes his parental rights. They are fostering him right now and are in family therapy with the boy. This is under the guidance of the childhood trauma center staff, and Lillian said the initial results are positive. I'm going to stay in touch with her and the staff at the trauma center, as I worry about that child. They may think I'm a real pain, but I don't care."

"The work of the sheriff is never done, is it?" said Osborne with a pat on her shoulder as they strolled along. "But this does sound like a good start for the boy. I think you're wise to stay in touch with those folks too."

"You know, Doc," Lew said after a few minutes had gone by, "I found Jane's behavior so unsettling that when she left my office, I did something I never thought I would do. I called Ed Pecore to let him know how sorry I felt for him, for his family, but especially for him, Doc. I realized he didn't know any of his niece's history, specifically how she had made all that money performing for the company posting the pornographic videos.

"All Ed knew about that young woman was that she was very attractive, had been financially successful, and was about to be married to a very wealthy older man. He was proud of her." Lew offered Osborne a sheepish smile. "Jane Willoughby's behavior struck me as so vile, I wanted to get rid of that feeling by doing something good. Even if it meant being nice to Ed. Am I a bad person or what?"

"C'mon, Lewellyn, you did a good thing. I'm sure Ed appreciated your sympathy. After all, he lost his sister, and now he's lost her daughter, his niece. Hey, let's turn here and head back to my place."

"Just in time," said Lew as they turned to walk back. "It's almost dark."

"My take on Bert and Jane Willoughby," said Osborne, "and keep in mind I've known Bert forever, is they enjoyed a family tradition of cheating people *and* each other."

"Didn't you tell me that Robin Steadman was astounded when she heard how much Bert had some of his patients paying him in cash in the belief they were getting a better deal than from their dental insurance?"

"Yes. When Robin learned how much cash Katherine must have grabbed from Bert's desk drawer, she realized what he had been up to—cheating the patient *and* cheating their insurers."

"I know Bert and Katherine had no scruples. But Jane too?"

"Mary Lee," said Osborne, referring to his late wife, "told me more than once that she was sure Jane cheated at bridge. Yep, family tradition."

* * *

Two hours later, as Lew and Osborne lay in his bed with the bedroom window ajar, the brisk night air hinted of snowy nights to come. Curling up next to Osborne, Lew listened, half-awake, to the whispers of white pine branches moving in the night breeze, the chucking of a busy chipmunk, and the hooting of a great horned owl. The night sounds of Loon Lake calmed her heart.

Osborne turned onto his side to pull her close. "Lewellyn, have I told you I love having you in my life?"

"No, Doc," she said sleepily. "*I* love having *you* in *my* life."

"Okay, okay," he whispered. "It's a draw. Sleep tight."

She let him have the last word.

Acknowledgments

A heartfelt thank-you to everyone who helped make *At the Edge of the Woods* read easily and look good. A special thank-you to my longtime editor (sometime publisher) and good friend, Ben LeRoy. Ben, your advice and support has been so appreciated over our years of working together. Thanks, too, to Sara Henry for impeccable editing, to Rachel Keith for excellent copyediting, and to Jerry Todd for his remarkable cover design. But none of this could have happened without the meticulous guidance from Melissa Rechter, Madeline Rathle, Rebecca Nelson, and Dulce Botello and the efforts of everyone on the Crooked Lane team—production and marketing—who have helped make *At the Edge of the Woods* possible.

You make me look good.